STONE COLD KILLER

"I told her to roll on her stomach. Then, I crawled on top of her, grabbed the gag, and I twisted it. She was out in seconds. Never moved a muscle. She just laid there until I cut off her breath. Then, I twisted it tighter and just held it there until her eyes bulged out and her face turned purple."

"Didn't that freak you out," Tina said, suddenly more aware just how cold-blooded this man really was. And, here she was, talking to him for the damn cops, listening to him get off as he related the details of Kathy's murder.

Wilson ignored the question.

"You ever murder anyone besides Kathy?"

"Yup," Wilson answered. "It's nothin' to me. You know I can ignore it like it isn't there—if the money is right."

Tina just nodded.

WHETHER IT'S A CRIME OF PASSION
OR
A COLD-BLOODED MURDER—
PINNACLE'S GOT THE TRUE STORY!

CRUEL SACRIFICE (884, $4.99)
by Aphrodite Jones
This is a tragic tale of twisted love and insane jealousy, occultism and sadistic ritual killing in small-town America . . . and of the young innocent who paid the ultimate price. One freezing night five teenage girls crowded into a car. By the end of the night, only four of them were alive. One of the most savage crimes in the history of Indiana, the four accused murderers were all girls under the age of eighteen!

BLOOD MONEY (773, $4.99)
by Clifford L. Linedecker
One winter day in Trail Creek, Indiana, seventy-four-year-old Elaine Witte left a Christmas party—and was never heard from again. Local authorities became suspicious when her widowed daughter-in-law, Hilma, and Hilma's two sons gave conflicting stories about her disappearance . . . then fled town. Driven by her insane greed for Witte's social security checks, Hilma had convinced her teenage son to kill his own grandmother with a crossbow, and then he fed her body parts to their dogs!

CONTRACT KILLER (788, $4.99)
by William Hoffman and Lake Headley
He knows where Jimmy Hoffa is buried—and who killed him. He knows who pulled the trigger on Joey Gallo. And now, Donald "Tony the Greek" Frankos—pimp, heroin dealer, loan shark and hit man for the mob—breaks his thirty year oath of silence and tells all. His incredible story reads like a who's who of the Mafia in America. Frankos has killed dozens of people in cold blood for thousands of dollars!

X-RATED (780, $4.99)
by David McCumber
Brothers Jim and Artie Mitchell were the undisputed porn kings of America. Multi-millionaires after such mega-hit flicks as BEHIND THE GREEN DOOR, theirs was a blood bond that survived battles with the mob and the Meese Commission, bitter divorces, and mind-numbing addictions. But their world exploded in tragedy when seemingly mild-mannered Jim gunned down his younger brother in cold blood. This is a riveting tale of a modern day Cain and Abel!

Available wherever paperbacks are sold, or order direct from the Publisher. Send cover price plus 50¢ per copy for mailing and handling to Penguin USA, P.O. Box 999, c/o Dept. 17109, Bergenfield, NJ 07621. Residents of New York and Tennessee must include sales tax. DO NOT SEND CASH.

WEB OF DECEIT

Gary C. King

PINNACLE BOOKS
WINDSOR PUBLISHING CORP.

PINNACLE BOOKS are published by

Windsor Publishing Corp.
850 Third Avenue
New York, NY 10022

First Printing: November, 1994

Printed in the United States of America

The names of some individuals in this book have been
changed. An asterisk appears after a fictitious name at the
time of its first occurrence.

For Teresita,
Forever the light of my life.

*The spider's touch, how
exquisitely fine!
Feels at each thread,
and lives along the line.*
　　　　　—Alexander Pope

Alieni appetins, sui profusus.
*Greedy for the property of others,
extravagant with his own.*
　　　　　—Sallust

Acknowledgements

The following people are much deserving of special acknowledgment for their work on this complicated case: Lloyd Davis, now retired; David Poppe; Michael Cline; Edward Van Horn; Wayne Irvin; J.T. Parr; J.R. Ellis; Donald Schuessler; and the many other fine officers and personnel of the Eugene, Oregon, Police Department who helped fit the pieces of this homicide puzzle into place. J. Pat Horton, former Lane County District Attorney, and Brian Barnes, former Lane County Deputy District Attorney, for prosecuting the bad guys and making certain that they remained behind bars for as long as possible. Also, thanks to F. Douglas Harcleroad, the current Lane County District Attorney, and his assistants, for taking the time out of their busy schedules to locate and bring out of storage the prosecution case files for me to examine.

I'd also like to sincerely thank the following people: Paul Dinas, Executive Editor at Pinnacle Books, for believing in the project; Susan Crawford of the Crawford Literary Agency, for negotiating the particulars; Beth Goehring, Editor, True Crime Book Club, for inducting me and my work into the ranks of book club readership; and Christofer Pierson, Managing Editor at *True Detective* magazine, for his continuing support, words of encouragement, wit, and wisdom.

For helping me to get the word out about my books, a special thank-you to: Jim Bosley, Mary Starrett, Janice Bangs, Peter Clem, and everyone else at *A.M. Northwest*, KATU-TV, Portland; Greg Carson, Brenda Braxton, and Rhonda Barton of *News at Noon*, KGW-TV, Portland; Julie Draper, Oregon Public Broadcasting; and in Seattle, Washington, Elisa Jaffe of *Northwest Afternoon*, KOMO-TV; and Gary Christienson for *The Jim French Show*, KIRO-Radio.

For actually getting the books out and for holding my hand at signings, thanks to: Roberta, Rick, Tom, Sally, and the rest of the gang at Fred N. Bay News, Portland; Ted Schwarz, wholesale sales representative for Penguin USA, Seattle; and all the other sales reps and booksellers across the country, without whom we, publishers, distributors, and authors alike, would soon all be out of business.

A very special thank-you to Sergeant Derrick Foxworth, Public Information Officer, Portland Police Bureau, and all the other men and women in blue who give unflaggingly of their time and who daily put their lives on the line to serve and protect the citizens of the City of Roses. *Be careful out there*, if I may borrow the phrase.

And last, but not least, much gratitude to Clemie Moody for all the thoughtfulness and kindness she has shown me and my family; and to Loreto Engles for your friendship and sincerity all these years, but most of all for just being you!

One

The city of Eugene, Oregon, the seat of Lane County, lies along the banks of the Willamette River, just off Interstate 5 in the western part of the Beaver State. Named for its first settler, Eugene Skinner, who arrived in the 1840s, the city has grown steadily since the arrival of the railroad in 1870 to become the state's second-largest city behind Portland, boasting a population of more than 112,000.

Idyllic in its natural beauty, Eugene is comfortably nestled in the fertile Willamette Valley, a nearly homogenous expanse of lowland accentuated by forest hills formed by the Cascade Mountains to the east and the Coast Range to the west. Occasionally at day's end, especially during the smoky late summer and early autumn months when farmers do most of their field burning, dusk eerily fills the hills and countryside around Eugene with a purple haze just before night draws down like a black cowl.

Midway between the state's northern and southern borders, some 110 miles south of Portland, Eugene, although it has seen better days, is still known as a center for timber and wood products industries, as well as for food-processing plants and home to the University of Oregon. Unfortunately, the city is also known as the setting for one of Oregon's most diabolical and fantastic contract murders ever.

Friday, July 6, 1984, proved to be a grueling and depressing day for Martha Roseann Chamberlin, a maid at Eugene's classy Valley River Inn, a four-star, 258-room establishment that faces the Willamette River and is noted for its fine dining. With the Fourth of July holiday now behind her, Martha had hoped that business would calm down, if only a little, at the hotel. But it hadn't. There weren't any vacancies for that Friday night, and by noon the hotel was booked throughout the weekend with tourists and businesspeople alike. As the summer sun continued to bear down on the Willamette Valley, raising the mercury to the mid-nineties, Martha sweated profusely as she pushed her utility cart toward the door to Room 305.

When she routinely checked her assignment sheet, she saw that Room 305 was listed as a checkout, which meant that she would have to strip the room and replace the soiled linen with fresh sheets and towels. After assembling the items she would need, Martha knocked on the door three times. Using her passkey, she opened the door several inches and dutifully called out,

"Maid," but did not enter the room. Although there was no response, Martha saw luggage on the floor near the door and heard that the television was on. Slightly embarrassed, thinking that she had nearly walked into a still-occupied room, Martha hastily closed the door and went on to the next room on her list.

It wasn't until 3 P.M. that Martha made it back to Room 305. She had stopped for lunch, and had decided to clean several other rooms before returning. The guest in 305, she reasoned, should have departed by now. It was one of the last rooms on her list of units to be cleaned that day, and Martha was by now in a hurry because she didn't want to put in any overtime, particularly on a Friday. Friday evening was her time for rest, relaxation, and sometimes recreation, even when she was scheduled to work over the weekend. Martha figured on Room 305 being an easy unit to finish, after which she could get on to her final rooms of the day.

Although she had every reason to believe that the occupant had checked out by now, Martha, out of habit, nonetheless identified herself again, then used her passkey and cautiously opened the door. Strangely, the luggage was still there, near the door where she had seen it earlier, and the TV was still on, causing her to wonder if the guest had decided to stay over for a second night. If the guest was indeed a stay-over, she thought, someone should at least have let her know.

"Do you need any maid service?" she called out as she pushed the door open the rest of the way. But, just like before, there was no response.

She had taken barely two steps into the room when she suddenly realized why no one had responded to her earlier. Across the room and directly in front of her lay the motionless body of a woman, naked from the waist down, sprawled facedown on the bed. When the realization that the woman might be dead struck her, Martha gasped and her whole body tightened as she backed stiffly out of the room. Nauseous, retching with fear and revulsion, Martha ran as fast as she could down the stairs to the hotel's administrative offices on the first floor.

"We've got to call the police!" she exclaimed, by now out of breath, her heart thumping harder against her ribcage. "There's a dead woman in Room 305!"

"Are you sure she's dead?" asked Patrick Hill*, the hotel's assistant manager.

"She's not moving, and she's naked!"

Hill, seeing the degree of Martha's distress, did not hesitate to make the call. Moments after he dialed 911, a dispatcher at the Lane County emergency communications center came on the line.

"Do you need fire, medical, or police assistance?" asked the calm, dispassionate voice on the other end of the line.

"Medical and police," the manager responded. Hill stayed on the line until the dispatcher had obtained all of the necessary information and assured him that emergency medical technicians from a nearby fire station were on the way and that a police officer would follow. He was instructed to make certain that nothing in the room would be disturbed.

Minutes later, Officer James Randolph Ellis of the Eugene Police Department, out on routine patrol and nearing the end of his day shift, heard the sketchy information as it crackled across his radio about the possible dead body at the hotel. There was not a lot of information, but Ellis heard that paramedics were already on the scene. Being in the vicinity he took the call and responded to the Valley River Inn, located at 1000 Valley River Way, right next to a mid-sized, tree-shrouded shopping mall aptly named the Valley River Center. So that he wouldn't arouse the curiosity of the guests who were checking in and out or unduly alarm anyone, Ellis didn't stop at the front desk but instead walked directly to the manager's office, from where he was directed to Room 305.

Two of the paramedics from the Eugene Fire Department who had arrived first were in the room next to 305 using the telephone when Ellis showed up, reporting that no lifesaving efforts were needed at their location. The partially clad female, one of them told their supervisor, was quite dead. The absence of respiration and the appearance of the body led Ellis to agree with the paramedics' conclusion. Ellis, following proper police procedure, secured the room and notified his dispatcher that he needed additional police department personnel at the scene, preferably a homicide unit, to investigate what he termed a suspicious death.

While waiting for additional help to arrive, Ellis checked the rooms on either side of Room 305 and found that both were empty. As part of his preliminary survey of the crime scene, Ellis determined that the two rooms across the hallway were occupied, but he had no way of knowing, yet, whether those guests had seen or heard anything suspicious. He noted the names of the two paramedics, as well as those of three additional fire department personnel who had entered the room prior to his arrival, all for the benefit of the investigators who would soon take over the case. As a footnote to his handwritten preliminary report he added that nothing, as far as he had been able to ascertain, had been touched or moved by anyone before he arrived and certainly not afterward.

Detective Lloyd Davis, a twenty-one-year veteran of the Eugene Police Department, was sitting behind his governmental steel-gray desk shuffling paperwork and thinking about going home when Sergeant Michael Cline stepped over to his desk in the large office that they shared, along with the rest of the unit's detectives, at a few minutes before 4 P.M. Davis, a detective for the past fourteen years who had been assigned to investigate crimes against persons, specifically the crimes of homicide, robbery, and rape, looked up at his colleague.

"Forget about going home today, Lloyd," Cline said. "I need you over at the Valley River Inn. We've got a suspicious death in Room 305. A housekeeper found the body, and she's pretty distraught. Officer Ellis is already on the scene."

Cline advised Davis, a kindly appearing, somewhat soft-spoken man with a reputation for leaving no stone unturned, that he would send additional uniformed officers to the scene to help keep it secure. Sergeant Cline assured Davis that he would also notify the district attorney's office and get a medical examiner out to the scene as soon as possible where he would join Davis later.

Davis knew from past experience that death investigations, even the simple ones, always took a lot of time and way too much paperwork. Not only was it getting close to quitting time, it was a Friday and he had been looking forward to having two days off, a luxury in his line of work. Davis pushed the stack of paperwork away from him as he stood up.

"There goes the weekend," he muttered to no one in particular as he grabbed a standard homicide kit on his way out of the office.

When Davis arrived at the hotel by himself ten minutes later, there were a number of people standing around in the hallway outside

Room 305, among them Officer Ellis. Ellis told Davis how he had responded to the call from the Valley River Inn regarding a possible deceased subject in Room 305, and briefed Davis on his preliminary examination and what he knew to have transpired both before and after his arrival. Davis officially took over the investigation at that point, and entered the room. Just as the maid had reported, the television was on, and Davis noted that several lights in the room were also on.

In an open closet to his left hung what he presumed to be some of the dead woman's clothes. Davis observed a light-blue skirt-and-blazer business suit, a black leather belt, a red satin-like top, and a pair of underpants, all of which hung on wooden hangers in the dressing area. A pair of black pumps and a pair of canvas navy blue walking shoes lay on the floor beneath them. A single piece of luggage, a small soft-sided overnight case, stood unzipped on the lower shelf in the closet and was visible from the room's entry door. The clothes, observed Davis, had been hung and placed very neatly.

While Davis was still making his preparatory observations, Sergeant Cline arrived. Davis was glad to see that Cline was accompanied by Donald Ray Schuessler, a laboratory technician who had worked for the Eugene Police Department for about six years. Schuessler's duties involved processing crime scenes and completing comparison analyses of certain types of physical evi-

dence, including fingerprints. Schuessler had
ridden along with Cline, both of whom were
followed into the room by Ken Champion, a
field investigator for the Lane County medical
examiner's office.

As they gathered around the bed, the investigators observed that the dead woman's body lay
across the width of the bed, not in a lengthwise
position in which a person would normally lie
when sleeping. A slightly damp hand towel from
the rack in the bathroom lay at the foot of the
bed. After viewing and photographing the body
exactly as it had been found, the investigators,
after Champion gave his okay, turned the corpse
over onto its back.

The deceased, they noted, was a brunette
woman with a slim figure who appeared to be
in her mid-to-late twenties. Her body was cool
to the touch, likely at or near room temperature.
Her hands, strangely, were clasped together near
her neck. She was wearing a diamond wedding
ring set on her left ring finger, and a silver ring
on her right ring finger. She was also wearing
a watch with a gold band on her right wrist.
There was no other jewelry on her body.

There was a small amount of blood, coagu-
lated and sticky, that had gravitated out of her
nose and mouth and had run down the sides
of her face, the cause of which could not be
immediately determined. On the bed near her
body lay a loose tuft of hair which, they observed, apparently had been torn from the

woman's scalp. Davis speculated that the tuft could have been torn loose during a struggle with an assailant, *if* it turned out that she had been murdered.

Davis observed that one of the bed pillows, lying near the corpse's head, had a small blood smear on it. There was an ashtray lying near the pillow, and a book of matches to the right of the woman's head. Schuessler's trained eye focused quickly on the ashtray, which had a smooth bottom surface that made it a good source for possible fingerprints. Schuessler made a note to seize, bag, and mark the ashtray, as well as the book of matches and the pillow, as soon as the room was sketched and photographed. As the investigators went through the room, they made notes to collect in a similar manner every item that held potential as evidence, again after the items were photographed and their locations duly noted on videotape.

As Davis observed the woman's partially nude body, clad only in a dark-colored mesh top and brassiere, the seasoned detective reflected that the woman had probably been quite attractive in life. Now, however, her appearance was ghoulish, made all the more so by the deep purple tone of the skin on the lower side of her body. Postmortem lividity, it was called, when the blood—all six pints of it, the average amount in an adult human being's body—is drawn by gravity to the lowermost regions of the body. Davis had seen it many times in his career. It was a sight that any homicide detective knows only too well.

Next to the bed on the floor, in front of a nightstand and slightly south of the woman's feet, which hung over the side of the bed, lay a pair of crumpled white slacks, presumably the dead woman's, that had been turned inside out during the process of being removed from her body by either herself or her assailant. Nearer to the nightstand, Davis observed, lay a Tampax tampon.

The tampon didn't look like it had been used, at least not for its intended purpose during a woman's menstrual period, because it didn't have any blood on it. Davis wondered if the tampon had been dropped there unnoticed by the woman. But then, a woman who by all appearances seemed so neat and clean wouldn't have simply left it there, he felt. If she had known that she dropped it, he felt that she would have picked it up and put it back in the box with the others. But where was the box? Not seeing it in the immediate area, Davis made a note to look for it when the room was processed more thoroughly. The tampon definitely seemed out of place to him, and seemed stranger still when he got down on his hands and knees to look at it more closely. He called Schuessler over, and pointed out that it appeared to be stained with a substance he could not immediately identify. Schuessler agreed that it was stained with *some-*

thing, and made a note to analyze it later at the lab.

As he continued his observations Davis found a black purse, unzipped, lying on top of the nightstand along with a pair of sunglasses. When he examined the purse he discovered that it did not contain any identification, nor did it contain a wallet, credit cards, or money. All he found inside it was a set of car keys.

A brown, soft leather satchel, apparently undisturbed, lay on a writing table next to the east wall of the room. Several official-looking documents, which the investigators believed the woman had carried into the room inside the valise, were spread out on top of a coffee table that sat in front of a sofa and next to a wicker side chair at the north end of the room. A full glass of what was soon determined to be water sat on a circular end table between the couch and the armchair, prompting Davis and the others to conclude that the woman had been doing some type of work prior to her demise and hadn't wanted to impair her mental faculties with anything stronger to drink.

Davis walked behind the wicker chair to a group of windows and a sliding glass door that led out onto a balcony. He pulled the curtains back and found that the door was locked. Like the front entrance door, he saw that it had not sustained any type of damage from someone trying to break in.

After a few minutes, Davis excused himself

from his colleagues and went downstairs to the registration desk. He needed to establish the dead woman's identity, the cornerstone or starting point from which everything else spiraled outward in a suspicious death investigation. It was also important to learn her identity so that her next of kin could be notified of her death.

When he examined the guest registration card for Room 305, he learned that Kathryn Ann Martini-Lissy had registered during the day of July 5, 1984, and planned to stay only one night. She had listed her home address as 128 Oswego Summit, Lake Oswego, Oregon, which Davis knew was an affluent suburb of Portland. According to the desk clerk who helped Davis, she had charged her room and other expenses to a credit card. As Davis scanned the guest registration card, he saw that she had indicated on the vehicle information section that she had driven a 1984 Datsun 300–Z, Oregon license plate KVC 525, to the hotel.

Davis went outside and easily found the 300–Z in the hotel's parking lot. It was the only 300–Z parked near the hotel. After he tried the keys that he had discovered in Room 305 and found that they fit the car, he felt reasonably certain that it belonged to the dead woman. A subsequent query to the Motor Vehicles Division confirmed that the car was registered to a Kathryn Ann Martini-Lissy, age twenty-six.

Davis next called Martha Chamberlin into an unoccupied conference room, where he asked

her to recount how she had found the body.
Martha, still visibly upset, told him there wasn't
much to tell, and explained the circumstances
that led up to her macabre discovery. She hadn't
seen anybody that she would consider a suspicious character during her shift, and she hadn't
noticed anyone loitering on the third floor.
Likewise, she hadn't heard any screams or com-
motion at any time during the day. She assured
him that she never touched or moved anything
in the room. She had left everything, she said,
just like she had found it.

Davis returned to the front desk, where he
inquired whether Mrs. Lissy had eaten any
meals in the hotel restaurant. The desk clerk
searched through the dining-room receipts, then
handed one that had been charged to Room 305
the previous evening over to Davis.

"May I take this with me?" Davis asked. "I'll
give you a receipt for it."

"Yes, of course."

Davis went to the hotel restaurant, where he
summoned the manager. When the manager appeared, Davis showed his identification and
handed him the ticket.

"Can you tell me who waited on this cus-
tomer?" Davis asked.

"Harry Dewitt Taylor, Jr.," the manager replied as he scanned the ticket. He was by now
aware of the body in Room 305 as was every
other hotel employee, and was eager to cooper-

ate with the police. "He's here now. Want to talk to him?"

"Yes," Davis said, as he followed the manager into the dining area. The manager spotted Taylor, then motioned him to come over to where they were standing.

"Mr. Taylor, did you wait on the person that this ticket is billed to?" Davis asked.

"Yes, I did," Taylor responded as he looked over the ticket. "Kathryn Martini-Lissy, she was the woman I waited on. This is the ticket, what she had, what she drank, everything that was purchased while I was waiting on her."

"That was yesterday, the fifth of July?"

"That's right. It was about six-thirty in the evening when she was first served. It shows the time right here, six-thirty-six. She had prime rib and espresso, and the prime rib comes with a salad and potato, vegetables, et cetera. She had two glasses of wine. One was a white one, the other was a red wine."

Taylor pointed out that the white wine was served shortly after her arrival, and that she was served the red wine at 7:02 P.M., when she received her meal.

"What time do you think she left the restaurant?" Davis asked.

"Around seven-thirty," Taylor said.

"Was anyone with her at that time?"

"Not that I could tell."

"Do you recall how she was dressed?"

"Nicely, in a business suit, very light-blue. It was almost a smoke-colored business suit."

"Did she have any paperwork with her?"

"Yes, she was writing on yellow paper, similar to a legal pad."

"You pretty sure about the time she left?"

"Yeah, pretty sure."

"Thanks. You've been very helpful." Davis retrieved the guest check and headed back upstairs.

When Davis rejoined his colleagues in Room 305 for another look around, he recalled that the tentatively identified dead woman had felt cold to the touch when they turned her corpse over earlier. That fact, when combined with the obvious postmortem lividity, Davis concluded, meant that she must have been dead for at least several hours prior to Martha Chamberlin's discovery of the body, perhaps even all night. Establishing a time of death, Davis knew, might shed some light on the case and help narrow down their field of inquiry. He knew that she had still been alive at 7:30 the night before. But twenty hours had elapsed from the time that Harry Taylor, Jr., the waiter, had served her dinner and the time that Martha Chamberlin had found her body. Based on such scant information, Davis resigned himself to the reality that there was just no way that they could determine the approximate time of death until they had more facts at their disposal.

If the woman had been murdered, as Davis's

gut feelings now led him to believe, the fact that her body was partially nude when she died strongly suggested sexual assault or rape as a possible motive. Davis also had to consider robbery as a possible motive, since he had found no money, checks, or credit cards in her room. But if she had been murdered, he continued to reason, why were there no signs of forced entry to the room, such as a broken door or door frame or smashed windows? Could she have opened the door to someone she knew? Or could the killer have somehow obtained a pass-key and had been lying in wait when she returned to her room? Or could she have opened the door to someone who was using a ruse, such as a hotel employee pretending to make a room-service delivery who had simply pushed his way into her room? If any one of those scenarios had occurred, there was certainly nothing to indicate that a struggle had occurred there, and that bothered him. How could she have died of violence without putting up a fight? Except for the tampon being out of place, the room was too neat and orderly for a struggle to have occurred there. The bedcoverings hadn't even been pulled back, making it a sure bet that Kathryn hadn't turned in for the night and that she had likely died fairly early on the evening of July 5.

At this point in the investigation, with nothing concrete enough to rule murder in or out yet, Davis had to consider whether the woman's cause of death could have resulted from any number of other causes, including an overdose of drugs, some type of seizure, or at least something in that vein. Although instinct told him that she had been murdered, officially he was still investigating only a suspicious death. He had no way of knowing just yet how far his investigation of Kathryn Ann Martini-Lissy's death would lead him and his colleagues into the depths of human degradation prevalent in Portland's netherworld, where the sordid plots and subplots of several individuals cavorting in drugs, kinky sex, prostitution, and conspiracy ran rampant. But he would know soon enough.

Two

Early in the investigation, Sergeant Michael Cline determined that Kathryn Ann Martini-Lissy was married to Michael David Lissy, her next of kin, at the time of her death. While Detective Lloyd Davis continued with his investigation at the Valley River Inn, Cline had telephoned Lissy to inform him that he had every reason to believe that his wife was dead. Cline asked Lissy to come to the Eugene Police Department as soon as possible, and requested that he bring with him several photographs of his wife. Lissy, who sounded pretty shaken up over the phone, to the point where he had to ask someone who was with him to finish the conversation for him, unhaltingly agreed to Cline's requests. Cline, meanwhile, called Davis back to the office so that they could go over all aspects of the case prior to Lissy's arrival.

It was nearly dark when Lissy arrived at City Hall, located at 777 Pearl Street in downtown Eugene, at 8:40 P.M., accompanied by his friend and neighbor, Al Blackman*, and his wife. The street lights cast an orange, shadowless glow over the trio as they got out of their car and walked up the steps to the building's front entrance. Davis and Cline met Lissy and his friends at the reception area, exchanged introductions and handshakes, then escorted them to their office. Along the way Davis observed that Lissy was a large man, built like a beer wagon. At approximately five feet ten inches tall and weighing about 240 pounds, Lissy seemed out of proportion to his wife. He guessed that opposites truly did attract.

"Did you bring the photographs of your wife, Mr. Lissy?" Davis asked.

"Yes," Lissy responded as he patted his shirt in an absent, searching gesture. After pulling the snapshots out of a pocket, he passed them with trembling, damply flaccid and thick-fingered hands over to the detective. Lissy looked upset and distraught, and at times appeared as if he might start crying at any moment. He watched intently as Davis looked at the photos.

"There's no doubt about it, Mr. Lissy," Davis said, shaking his head as he looked up from the photos. "Your wife is the deceased person we found in the hotel room. I'm very sorry."

Lissy appeared to be in shock when he first heard Davis's words, as if he had expected the detective to tell him that it had all been a mistake and that it *wasn't* his wife that had been found dead in Room 305. Then, after the reality of it all seemed to settle in, he brought a hand to his brow and began crying. His friends did what they could to console him as Davis and Cline looked on in silence, observing what they perceived to be clearly a sorrowful, grieving husband carrying on over the death of his beloved wife. Davis pushed a box of Kleenex toward him.

"Mr. Lissy," Davis said after giving Lissy a few minutes to try and compose himself. "I can understand how you must be feeling at a time like this, and I truly sympathize with you. But, as painful as your loss is, I must ask you some questions, particularly questions that deal with background information about your wife. Some of the questions will be difficult and painful. Do you feel up to answering them at this time?"

"Go ahead and ask them," Lissy said between sobs, nodding that he could respond to Davis's queries.

"Was Kathryn a heavy drinker?" Davis asked.

"No. Kathy was only a social drinker," Lissy said. Lissy pointed out that his wife was more commonly called Kathy. She preferred to be called Kathy, he said, because she thought Kathryn sounded too formal.

"Was Kathy ever involved with narcotics of any kind?"

"Why, yes, she was," Lissy replied without hesitation. "Whenever she would come to Eugene, she would buy cocaine," he volunteered.

Lissy's answer, or perhaps just the blunt abruptness of it, seemed to surprise Davis. Although he didn't tell Lissy, Davis didn't think Kathy seemed like the type of person who would have used illegal drugs. There seemed to be an orderliness to her life, based on Davis's early perception, and not the kind of chaos that seemed to prevail in the lives of so many drug users he had dealt with in his profession over the years. Besides, they hadn't found any signs of illicit drugs in Kathy's room, at least not yet.

"How much cocaine did she normally buy?" asked the detective.

"Oh, usually just a gram," Lissy said. Davis knew that the cost for a gram of coke ranged from $100 to $125, rarely higher, and that it was easily obtainable in Eugene if one knew the right people.

"Was her use of cocaine frequent or only occasional?"

"She purchased cocaine almost every time she came to Eugene," Lissy said, still sniffling. He explained that she thought the quality of cocaine in Eugene was better than it was in the Portland area.

"How much money was she carrying with her?"

"Approximately eight hundred dollars, maybe more. I gave her five hundred dollars to put in the bank two or three days ago, then gave her another three hundred the night before she left. She may have also had some of her own money with her."

"Do you know if Kathy ever used any other types of drugs?"

"Yeah. She used MDA occasionally."

MDA, Davis knew, was an amphetamine-based hallucinogen, a so-called synthetic "designer drug," the active ingredient of which is 34–methylenedioxyamphetamine. Sometimes called MDA, MMDA, or MDM, the drug is more often referred to on the streets as Adam, Love Drug, Ecstasy, and XTC. Again, MDA didn't seem like the type of thing with which Kathryn Lissy would have gotten involved. But then, he kept telling himself, he really didn't know much about her yet, and often, when all was said and done, the subjects of his investigations were not always what they seemed at a probe's outset.

"Do you know who Kathy obtained these drugs from?"

"Sometimes she got them from one of the girls that worked in one of my diving shops. I don't know her name."

"What do you do for a living?" Davis asked, now curious and seeing an easy opening to delve deeper into Lissy's life.

Lissy calmly explained that he ran his own business, Valley Windsurfing and Scuba Shops. There were two shops, actually, located in different areas of Portland. One was on Northeast Broadway in Portland's Hollywood District and the other on Southwest Barbur Boulevard, which Lissy dubbed Valley I and Valley II, respectively. He sold windsurfing and scuba-diving equipment, and provided certification classes for the latter. That, he explained, was how he and Kathy had first met.

It was in May 1983, when Kathy was still new to the Portland area, that she decided to sign up for scuba-diving lessons from Lissy, who was then thirty-four. She didn't know very many people in town, especially anyone who was qualified to be her partner for scuba-diving certification classes. Lissy, after taking one look at her, volunteered, and their relationship blossomed from there, he said.

"Why was Kathy in Eugene?" Davis wanted to know.

"She was here on business," he said, "a trip that was part of her job." He explained that Kathy had been a commercial loan officer for the Portland branch of the Bank of Boston, and that she had planned to stay only one night and then return on July 6.

"When did you last hear from Kathy?"

"She called and left a message on the answering machine at about noon."

"At noon on July fifth?"

"Yes." Lissy explained that he had called her back, and that she had told him that the reason she called was that she had left her toothpaste on the counter at home. "I told her to just go out and buy some more." Toothpaste seemed like such a lame reason to call home about, but Davis kept his thoughts to himself about that.

"I'm sorry to have to ask this, but I must. Did Kathy have any male friends that you know of whom she might have been visiting while in Eugene?"

Lissy didn't reply immediately. He sat silent for a moment, as if hesitant about vocalizing his next thought. He shifted uneasily in his chair, then indicated that he needed to go to the restroom. Davis got up and walked down the hall with him. On the way, Lissy indicated that the real reason he wanted to get out of the room was that he didn't want the Blackmans—his and Kathy's friends—to hear what he was about to say.

"Kathy and I had a very open relationship," Lissy said slowly, in a flat inflectionless voice, feeling his way and searching for the right words. "She had boyfriends, and I had girl-friends."

Despite Lissy's apparent candor, Davis sensed a certain remoteness about him, like he had deliberately constructed a barrier that no one could penetrate. Although he didn't know what it was, Davis saw something flickering far back in Lissy's eyes. He didn't know if it had something to do with Lissy's cool, well-bred manner, or if what he saw was sorrow, fear, or perhaps deception. Lissy, sensing that he was being assessed, continued talking.

Neither he nor his wife had had any problems over the arrangement, Lissy said. The Blackmans, he stressed, weren't aware of any of this, and he didn't want to unduly shock them by telling Davis about it in their presence. He said that Kathy had a former lover named Jay, but he didn't know the man's last name. He thought the man lived in the Eugene area, but didn't have an address. The picture that Davis was receiving from Lissy's statements was that of a promiscuous bank officer who also used drugs, but he didn't make any comments about it. He just asked the questions, took notes of the answers, and observed.

When they returned to Davis's office, the detective asked Lissy about other types of property that Kathy might have had with her. Lissy said that Kathy always wore a diamond pendant necklace, and always carried credit cards with her. She usually carried a BankAmericard or Mastercard, a couple of American Express cards, and a Bank of Boston card. Lissy said that Kathy used her maiden name of Martini on some of the cards, and Martini-Lissy as the last name on others, but he wasn't sure which names were used on which accounts. She carried the credit cards, along with an Oregon driver's license, in a dark-blue or black wallet. She also never went anywhere without her address book.

"We never found any of those items in Kathy's room at the Valley River Inn," Davis said matter-of-factly.

Davis explained that he didn't yet know if foul play was involved in Kathy's death or not, but indicated that he was suspicious that it was. If it turned out that foul play was involved, he said he would have to try and determine a motive. Lissy offered that perhaps Kathy had been killed over a drug deal that had gone awry, or an affair that had gotten out of hand. Lissy, strangely, seemed to have an answer for everything during his time of grief. Davis simply said that it was standard procedure to treat all dead bodies as a homicide until the death in question had been determined to be otherwise.

"Can you account for your whereabouts on July fifth?" Davis asked in his next breath.

The question caught Lissy off guard, and obviously startled him. As cruel and uncaring as it may seem, that had been Davis's intention. The spouse of a murder victim or of someone who had died suspiciously is nearly always viewed as the number one suspect until cleared, and in Davis's mind Lissy was no exception.

"I was probably at or between my two stores from about nine-forty-five in the morning until about six-thirty at night," Lissy said. He explained that at about 6:30 P.M., he and one of his employees, Roy Graham*, had gone to Walter Mitty's, a tavern and lunch-type restaurant located near one of his shops. Lissy said that they had drinks and hors d'oeuvres together, and after finishing their drinks he and Roy parted company and had gone their separate ways.

On his way home, Lissy said, he had stopped over at Al Blackman's house and talked to him for a short time, then went on home and passed out. He said he thought he had arrived home at about 9:30 to 9:45 P.M., but wasn't certain. He said he didn't wake up until the next morning at about 9:30 A.M. Lissy was adamant that he had not been in Eugene on July 5 or July 6 until he drove down at Sergeant Cline's request.

At the conclusion of the interview, Davis thanked Lissy for his time and again offered his condolences. The detective added that it would be necessary for him to track Kathy's missing credit cards, and asked that Lissy call him when he got back to Portland to provide him with the specific information about the cards, such as the names they were issued under and the account numbers. Lissy assured him that he would. Davis, likewise, promised that he would get in touch with Lissy following the autopsy, scheduled for the next morning.

Three

It was 9 A.M. the next day, July 7, a Saturday, when Detective Lloyd Davis, Detective David Poppe, his younger partner, and laboratory technician Donald Schuessler arrived at 1255 Hillyard Street. Eugene's Sacred Heart Hospital, which houses Lane County's only morgue facility, is located at that address. Davis, Poppe, and Schuessler were there to witness the definitive autopsy on Kathryn Martini-Lissy's body, which would be performed by Dr. Edward F. Wilson, a physician-pathologist who had served as Lane County's medical examiner for the past fourteen years.

The state of Oregon has long had a death investigation law on its books which requires an investigation into homicides, suicides, accidents, and suspicious deaths, such as Martini-Lissy's, by autopsy. An autopsy, of course, involves the external and internal examination of the body, including all of its cavities, as well as the collection of blood and other samples for use as evidence. Davis, Poppe, and Schuessler had been to the morgue many times before and knew their way to its location in the hospital's basement, the "dregs" of the six-story medical facility. Wilson was already there, as was one of his assistants.

Dr. Wilson, a 1963 graduate of Yale Medical School, completed his residency at Johns Hopkins Hospital in Baltimore, Maryland. Afterward he served as assistant state medical examiner in Maryland for two years and then as the state medical examiner in Utah for another two years. He was, without question, well-qualified to assume the duties of Lane County's medical examiner when he arrived in Eugene in 1971. He and many of the lawmen from Lane County and the Eugene Police Department had gotten to know each other quite well over the years.

Wilson greeted the investigators with a wave of his hand, beckoning them over to the stainless-steel autopsy table where Kathy's body lay on its back. Prior to getting underway, Wilson pointed out for the record that the body remained as it had been found, clad only in a dark knit blouse, brassiere, a wristwatch, and two rings. Those items were eventually removed before Wilson began the autopsy, after Schuessler photographed the body again. Schuessler would take additional photographs throughout the procedure.

Beginning with the corpse's head, Wilson pointed out a two-inch area of scalp and hair that was missing from the left side, about one and three-quarter inches above the ear. He noted that the face was very congested and swollen, much more so than the rest of the body. There was hemorrhaging in the eyelids and in the white of the eyes the size of pinheads and pinpoints, which became heavy and solid nearer the eye sockets, and there were two small abrasions on the right side of the face, near the mouth. There was a large "Y"-shaped abrasion located about two inches behind the left earlobe, which interested Wilson and the investigators immensely.

"The external exam suggests that asphyxiation due to strangulation should be considered as the cause of death," Wilson dictated for the official report. Because no fingernail marks were found on the outside of the neck, which would indicate manual strangulation with the hands, Wilson felt that a ligature of some sort had been used to strangle her.

In an attempt to observe whether delineation from a ligature was present but unseen by an unaided eye, an assistant pathologist positioned a black light over the body near the neck according to Wilson's instructions. They all knew that ligature marks, if any were present, often showed up brightly under a black light. When the normal lights were brought down, however, there were no signs of blanching to the naked eye that would suggest strangulation by ligature. Nonetheless, Wilson's gut feelings told him that Kathy was a homicide victim, and he vowed that he would demonstrate before the conclusion of the autopsy that she had been strangled.

Next, Wilson examined the various orifices of Kathy's body to see if any evidence could be extracted from the cavities. Using cotton swabs, he collected specimens of the moisture inside the victim's mouth, vagina, and rectum, and handed them over to Schuessler who would study them later at the crime lab. While collecting the specimens, Wilson noticed an injury inside Kathy's vaginal tract. It was a possible abrasion, he pointed out to the investigators, three-sixteenths of an inch wide by one-sixteenth of an inch long on the posterior wall at the entrance to the vagina. As he removed a piece of tissue to examine under a microscope, Wilson explained that an abrasion was a superficial loss of the epidermis, the outermost layer of skin. When he examined the sample microscopically, he confirmed that it was indeed an abrasion, but only a slight one.

As they wondered about the possible causes for the abrasion, Wilson told Davis, Poppe, and Schuessler that it was compatible with a forcible attempt at sexual intercourse. He also did not dismiss the possibility that it could have been caused by the attempted penetration of an inanimate, nonanatomical object such as a dildo. But there was no way that he could determine with any degree of certainty what had caused the injury, and he told them so. He could only make educated guesses based on the degree and nature of the injury.

Wilson discovered two other small abrasions, both on the corpse's right hip. One was a quarter-inch in size and the other an eighth of an inch. It was possible, he reasoned, that the injuries could have been sustained in a struggle with the attacker, but, as with the vaginal abrasion, he could not be certain.

Davis told Wilson about finding the tampon inside the victim's room, how they had tossed ideas off one another about its possible significance, and how they had not found any signs that Kathy had been menstruating. When he checked, the medical examiner could find no evidence of menstruation.

When informed that Kathy's death might be related to a cocaine deal, Wilson suggested that people sometimes pack illegal drugs into their body orifices to avoid detection if arrested. Since Kathy was a potential buyer, according to what her husband had told Davis the night before, they theorized that it was possible that another woman, perhaps a drug dealer herself or a drug dealer's "bag bitch," had put a bag of cocaine up her vagina and had held it in place with the tampon until it was time to make the delivery to Kathy. But if that had been the case, where was the cocaine now? None was found in Kathy's room, and there were no other signs, such as cocaine paraphernalia, that any had even been used there.

It was possible, they continued to theorize, that someone had brought cocaine to Kathy's room

but for some reason had also taken it away. Kathy
may have angered the drug dealer somehow, perhaps by arguing about the price or the cocaine's
quality, which had resulted in an altercation and
Kathy's death. It was also possible that the drug
dealer had glimpsed the amount of cash that
Kathy was believed to have been carrying when
she opened her purse to pay him or her for the
cocaine and had made a spur of the moment decision to rob and kill Kathy simply for her money.
If the dealer had been accompanied by a woman
who was carrying the cocaine inside her vagina,
the woman, hypothetically, could have assisted
him after the deal went awry by holding Kathy
immobile while he strangled her. That could explain why there were no signs of a struggle inside
Kathy's hotel room. As the autopsy proceeded,
Davis, Poppe, Schuessler, and Wilson continued
bouncing ideas off one another about what *could*
have happened inside Room 305, but failed to
reach any concrete conclusions as to why Kathy
had been killed.

When Wilson surgically removed the scalp, he
discovered a large contusion or bruise beneath
the spot where the "Y"-shaped abrasion appeared on the outside. When they began discussing the degree of force that would be necessary
to cause that type of injury, Wilson said it could
have been caused by someone swinging something intentionally with their hand, such as a belt,
that would leave a mark on the skin upon impact.
They also considered that the "Y"-shaped mark

and bruising could have been caused by a belt buckle or some other type of metal object attached to a ligature that had been subjected to continued or prolonged pressure, such as that which would be caused by someone pulling or tightening it around the victim's neck.

During the internal examination, which included an examination of the neck structures, Wilson discovered a wide mark or discoloration on the underside of the skin and in the muscles and the thyroid gland. He dissected the neck muscles one-by-one, and found hemorrhaging approximately two inches wide from top to bottom. The dimensions of the hemorrhaging were consistent with those of a wide object, such as a belt.

After the torso was opened in the usual manner, Wilson looked at the contents of the stomach to try and figure out if part or all of Kathy's last meal was still there or had passed on to the duodenum. He pulled out a piece of meat at one point.

"She didn't chew her food very good," Wilson said as he placed the meat in a stainless-steel pan.

"When do you think she died, Doc?" Davis asked.

Wilson explained that it takes from four to six hours for the contents of the stomach of an average, healthy person to pass on to the intestines. In Kathy's case, he pointed out, much of her meal was still in her stomach.

"This woman died within a few hours, perhaps only one to two hours, after she ate," Wilson said.

That would mean, Davis reasoned, that Kathy had been killed as early as 8:30 or 9:30 P.M. on July 5, provided that she had in fact finished dinner by 7:30 P.M. like the waiter had told him.

Davis called Michael Lissy later that day to obtain the account numbers of the credit cards Kathy was believed to have been carrying when she went to Eugene. Lissy, crackling a piece of paper as he unfolded it, told him that he had the numbers. Kathy always carried a Bank of Boston credit card, he said, number 361197, in the name of Kathryn A. Martini. She also carried two American Express cards—one in the name of Kathryn Martini numbered 378240067931002, and the other in the name of Kathryn Martini-Lissy numbered 372045745912001.

When Lissy finished reading off the information, Davis explained that the autopsy had been completed. Anticipating that Lissy would likely have questions, he was quick to point out that he hadn't received a copy of the report yet and didn't want to discuss the medical examiner's findings until he had a copy of the report in hand. Davis then asked him how he wanted to handle the disposition of his wife's body and Lissy, in a weak voice, told Davis that he wanted her body cremated. Davis assured him that he would pass the information on to the medical examiner who would, in turn, provide it to the receiving mortuary.

"We need to talk some more before we can finish up with this business," Davis said. "Sergeant Cline and I are planning to drive up to your place later this afternoon. Is that okay with you?"

"Yeah, sure," Lissy said. He provided directions on how to get to his Lake Oswego condo, and Davis told him that he and Cline would be there between 5 and 6 P.M.

Davis and Cline left Eugene at 3:20 P.M. The northbound traffic on Interstate 5 was moderate at that time of the day and they made good time driving the legal speed limit. Since it was a Saturday, rush-hour traffic wouldn't be a problem at any of the communities between Eugene and Lake Oswego.

Not all that familiar with Lake Oswego, Davis and Cline had difficulty locating 128 Oswego Summit, the address for Lissy's condo, when they arrived. Rather than waste valuable time searching for it, they returned to a 7–Eleven they recalled seeing when they first drove into town. There was a telephone booth on a street corner near the store from where Davis could call Lissy for more precise directions. As luck would have it, however, Davis never had to make the call. He saw Lissy and Al Blackman, just as he was about to enter the phone booth. They had come out of the 7–Eleven and climbed into

Lissy's blue Chevy van, bearing Oregon license plate CTL 507. Davis rushed over and made his presence known to Lissy, after which he and Cline followed Lissy and Blackman to the condo.

It was 5:15 P.M. when they arrived a few minutes later. In addition to Blackman, Lissy's stepfather and mother were there, as were Lissy's former wife, Elise Dunn,* and a pastor from a local church. After introductions were completed, Lissy escorted the two investigators into his den, which was out of sight and earshot of the others. Lissy appeared tired, and bags had begun to form beneath his eyes. After a few moments Lissy broke the silence.

"Did you find out if Kathy was murdered or not?" he asked.

"Yes, she was murdered," Davis replied in a low, sympathetic voice. Davis did not offer, however, nor was he asked, how Kathy had been killed.

Davis calmly explained that Kathy's body was nude from the waist down when discovered, and described how her slacks had been removed and were lying on the floor. He also told him about the tampon, but did not try to elicit a response from Lissy about it at that time.

"How would Kathy normally undress?" Davis asked. "Would she hang up her pants or leave them lying on the floor?"

"She was very neat," Lissy said. "She always hung up her clothing. She would never leave any of her clothes lying on the floor."

"How long had you known Kathy?"

"About a year," Lissy answered. "Shortly after we met, I moved into her apartment and we began living together."

"How many trips did Kathy normally make to Eugene in a month?"

"She made approximately one trip a month, on business."

"Did Kathy have anyone in particular that she was afraid of or had seemed concerned about? You know, someone she feared might cause her harm or something like that?"

"No one that I can think of," Lissy said. Lissy did mention, however, a couple of male friends of Kathy's. One, he said, was named Hamna. He didn't know the man's first name, and he said he wasn't certain that the spelling of his last name was correct. The other man was named Phil—a guy Kathy had gone out with prior to her marriage to Lissy—but Lissy didn't know Phil's last name.

At 5:45 P.M., while Davis was taking notes of Lissy's answers, another person, a man, joined them in the den. Lissy introduced him as Michael Sturgeon, his attorney. Davis, for one fleeting moment, wondered why Lissy felt it was necessary to have his attorney present. Davis quickly put the thought out of his mind for the time being, then asked Sturgeon if he had any objections about him questioning Lissy.

"Go ahead and talk to him," Sturgeon said. "Ask any questions you'd like."

"Do you have any cocaine in the house?" Davis asked.

"No, I do not," Lissy responded.

Davis, sensing a slight amount of hostility to his abrupt question, promptly clarified his question by saying he was interested in some paper fold. A gram of cocaine, he said, is often sold in folded paper.

"We were thinking if Kathy had been murdered by a coke connection," Davis said, "we could have the paper fold to process for fingerprints, which might help our investigation."

"Kathy kept her coke in a vial," Lissy said, "and I don't know where it is."

"Do you use cocaine, Mr. Lissy?" Davis asked.

"Sometimes," he said. "But not much. Kathy was a frequent user, though." Lissy explained that, prior to marrying Kathy, he ran in different circles. After their marriage he often ended up going to parties with Kathy, and there was usually a large amount of cocaine available. At one party, he said he saw what he thought to be approximately $10,000 worth of coke on a table.

Davis turned the line of questioning back toward Lissy's relationship with Kathy. Lissy reiterated much of what he had told Davis the night before in Eugene, but something kept gnawing at Davis to keep pushing. Was their sex good together? he asked. Was there anything of a sexual nature to cause them any marital discord, such as the open relationship they had supposedly mutually agreed upon?

"Two weeks ago," Lissy said with some difficulty, "we became aware that we had VD. I don't know if I gave it to Kathy through one of my extramarital affairs, or if she gave it to me through one of hers."

"When was the last time you had sex with your wife?" Davis asked.

"The night of July fourth," Lissy said. "We had sexual intercourse three or four times."

While Davis mulled over what Lissy had said, particularly about him and Kathy having contracted a venereal disease, he found himself wishing that a bacteriological exam had been performed on Kathy's body at the time of autopsy. But he would soon find out that it was too late to have such an examination performed, now. The morgue, he would learn upon his return to Eugene, had released her body to a mortuary that afternoon and it had already been cremated according to Lissy's wishes.

If she had truly had a venereal disease, Davis now reasoned, that might account for the mysterious tampon in her room. Secretions form in the vagina of a woman with such a disease, and there would normally be some discharge. Although Kathy hadn't been menstruating, she might have used the tampon to catch the discharge from whatever disease she had contracted, and the tampon may have had no bearing whatsoever on a possible cocaine connection. Davis suddenly realized that he may have been barking up the wrong tree.

"Do you know what type of life insurance Kathy had?" Davis asked, fishing.

"I don't know," Lissy calmly replied. "I hadn't even thought about it. I don't know if she had any life insurance at all."

Four

Kathryn Ann Martini was born on April 28, 1958, a Monday, to a good, respectable New York family. One of three girls in her family, Kathy was raised just outside of New York City by loving and caring parents who taught her and her sisters strong personal values, such as to always be honest, caring, and giving. Kathy's parents were very proud of her, and nearly always supported whatever she did. She in turn eventually fulfilled their hopes and dreams. By the time she had finished high school, they firmly believed that she would turn out the way that most parents hope and pray their children will. She had given them no reason to believe otherwise.

After graduation from high school, Kathy went on to study economics at Yale University. Pursuing swimming as an extracurricular activity that would not detract her from her academic aspirations, Kathy soon joined the Ivy League university's women's varsity swim team as a diver. Exhibiting brilliance in her studies and mastery in her swimming, Kathy was nonetheless kind of an all-around person, well-liked by her classmates. At one point she began a women's awareness group at the university, and in her spare time, what little there was, she volunteered as a "Big Sister" in New Haven, Connecticut, and gave freely of her time at the New Haven YWCA.

Following graduation from Yale, Kathy was hired by the First National Bank of Boston and was one of only a small number of women who were accepted into that financial institution's loan officer training program. After successfully completing the bank's curriculum in the early part of 1982, she was transferred to the other side of the country to Portland, where she became one of the bank's first female commercial loan officers specializing in transactions in excess of $500,000. Then twenty-four, Kathy was an attractive brunette, intelligent, ambitious, and highly motivated to succeed in life. Her mentors instinctively knew that she had all the traits of a successful, up-and-coming young businesswoman in the highly competitive banking profession.

Shortly after her arrival in Oregon, Kathy joined the Network of Business and Professional Women of Portland, to which she served on various functions and in keeping with her well-established trait gave generously of her time. In a display of appreciation for all of her hard work, not to mention being desirous of the continuance of her skills and abilities, the group soon elected her as their president, one of the youngest ever.

"I looked at her and said, 'Wow, this is an example of what women can do today,' " said Carole F. Barkley, one of the group's vice presidents, soon after meeting Kathy. "She's what you would visualize if you had to pick a representative of a successful, young businessperson today. Everything in her life seemed golden."

Indeed, life *seemed* golden for Kathy. She enjoyed a good salary from her job, traveled with all expenses paid, drove an expensive sports car, and lived in a luxurious condominium in the affluent Portland suburb of Lake Oswego that overlooked the lake after which the town was named. More accomplished and self-guided than most people of her age, Kathy moved faster than many of her professional peers. Because of her many successes and mature mannerisms, she impressed people as seeming older than she actually was. It was because of her maturity, perhaps, that she attracted and sometimes chose to date slightly older men.

In May 1983, while still relatively new to the Portland area, Kathy's life took a dramatic turn when she decided to continue aquatics studies and signed up to take scuba-diving lessons at one of the Valley Windsurfing and Scuba Shops. That's where she met thirty-four-year old Michael David Lissy, an aquatic supplies businessman and certified scuba-diving instructor. Kathy didn't know anyone in town who could teach her scuba-diving, so Michael eagerly offered to be her partner for the certification classes.

Lissy, charismatic and full of charm, soon cast a spell of sorts upon her. Kathy fell instantly in love with him, and the two became seemingly inseparable. They dated frequently, often seeing each other every day. They began living together in July 1983, and were married the following January, little more than a month after Michael had obtained a divorce from his third wife, Elise. He soon made Kathy the president of his business.

Michael, in one of his boastful moods, had told Kathy that he had graduated from Harvard and Oxford universities. This had impressed his new bride, and she was proud to be married to a highly educated, successful businessman. He also told her that he was going to head a dive for the National Geographic Society, and that he held diving contracts with the Department of Defense and the Department of State. Kathy, overwhelmed and fascinated, began telling her friends that Michael would get mysterious telephone calls in the middle of the night, and would have to go to another room to talk about "top secret" diving plans he had made with the government. She was initially intrigued by her husband's mysteriousness and, her friends would later say, she truly believed that she had found the man of her dreams.

"Kathy was really in love with Michael," said Kathleen Kolstad, one of Kathy's best friends. "She really believed in him. My husband and I met him just before they got married. Michael was quite the charmer."

Never, not even for an instant, said her friends, did Kathy envision that her pipe dream would come to an abrupt end, a dead halt, because of the evil plotting and sinister actions of another. When informed of Kathy's untimely death, none of her friends and acquaintances could think of anyone who would want to do her harm.

In their reconstruction of Kathy's final hours alive, Detectives Lloyd Davis and David Poppe knew that, early on Thursday morning, July 5, Kathy had packed a small suitcase, ate a light breakfast, then loaded the suitcase into her car. Looking at the view outside her and Lissy's condo, they knew that she must have gazed, even if only momentarily, across the lake that her home overlooked after she had backed out of the garage. Because of her business acumen and discipline, she must have also gone over in her mind the outline of her planned, overnight business trip to Eugene, probably never considering that she might not return to her world of success and the man of her dreams as she zoomed on down Interstate 5 that fateful morning.

As best as Davis and Poppe could tell, Kathy arrived in Eugene about two hours after leaving home and promptly checked into the room that she had reserved at the Valley River Inn. They confirmed that, after she had checked in, Kathy had attended a business meeting, a luncheon, another business meeting in the afternoon, and then returned to her room to get some rest. It had all been part of her ordinary duties to call on accounts and create new business for the bank. Her position, by its very nature, put her in close professional contact with people of high stature and financial well-being in the business community. Later, after recuperating from the business affairs of the day, she had eaten dinner alone in the hotel's restaurant, and had even brought some of her work with her to the dining table. After eating her meal and drinking two glasses of wine while looking over some documents, Kathy had, as far as the detectives had been able to determine, gone straight back to her room to retire for the night. She had not been seen by anybody again until hotel maid Martha Chamberlin discovered her body the next afternoon.

In the days and weeks that followed, Davis and Poppe would interview all of Kathy's known business associates in Portland and Eugene, as well as many who lived and worked on the East Coast, talk with relatives and all of her known friends and acquaintances, virtually everyone who knew her even remotely. They would naturally trace her movements in Eugene as far as they could, if they hadn't already done so, and more than 150 hotel employees would be questioned either by them or the many other law officers working on the case.

A reward fund was promptly established by the Network of Business and Professional Women of Portland whose members, understandably, were outraged over Kathy's murder. Within a matter of days, the reward fund topped $10,000.

"It (the money) came from people who cared about Kathy all over the country . . . a tremendous response. . . . It seems everyone who knew her is very concerned," said a network member and personal friend of Kathy's. However, despite the size of the reward offer, there were no takers and Kathy's killer remained at large.

Five

"He did it! Oh, my God, he did it!" exclaimed Molly Griggs, seventeen, after reading a newspaper article on Monday morning, July 9, 1984, about Kathryn Martini-Lissy's murder at the Valley River Inn. Molly was hysterical and began crying as she continued to exclaim, over and over, "He did it!"

"Did what?" asked David, her boyfriend. "Who did what?" It took Molly nearly ten minutes to calm down to the point where she could explain to David what she was so upset about. Molly, shaking with trepidation and fear, said that she had met a man named Michael David Lissy a few months earlier in downtown Portland, and that Lissy had asked her to help him find a hit man to kill a young woman. David, shocked and himself fearful over what Molly had told him, advised Molly to contact the Eugene Police Department, which she did a few minutes later after composing herself. At Molly's request, David dialed the number and got Detective Davis on the line. After briefly explaining that his girlfriend might have some important information about the Martini-Lissy homicide, he handed the phone to Molly.

As Molly recounted her story of reading about Kathy's murder in the newspaper, Davis sensed and later confirmed that Molly was a troubled kid who had somehow gotten on the wrong track and found herself in circumstances which she now regretted, as so often happens to people in virtually all walks of life. A period of her troubled life, he deduced from the information she conveyed, involved the Third Avenue and Taylor Street area of downtown Portland, from where the sordid activities of prostitution, drug usage, and dope peddling generated. It was through people involved with such activities that Molly had come to know Michael Lissy very well.

"But what makes you think he was involved in the death of his wife?" Davis asked.

"Because what I read was the same manner of death that he had described to me, and because she was young, because it fit exactly the same description that he had given me previously."

In backing up her story a bit, Molly indicated that a month earlier, in June, Lissy had been involved in a scheme in which he was trying to intimidate a woman, though Molly didn't know the woman's identity. But the scheme had involved him hiring Molly, in which he had paid her $100 for each of three telephone calls that Molly had made to this mystery woman. Basically, the calls were of a threatening nature that demanded that the woman play ball with Lissy and keep her mouth shut, do what Lissy wanted her to do or he would expose some of her previous activities that she wasn't proud of. Molly didn't know what it was that Lissy wanted the woman to do, nor did she know what the "previous activities" referred to, but it had sounded to Molly like Lissy's actions were a form of blackmail and intimidation.

During the process of arranging to make the threatening calls, Lissy, after he had gotten to know her and had become comfortable with her, had told Molly that he needed her help in performing other tasks, including that he wanted to have a woman strangled. He didn't tell her *who* he wanted strangled, only that it was a young woman, that he would provide a time and place where the killing was to occur, and that he needed it done very soon. She explained that Lissy had said that he would be willing to pay $5,000 to the killer.

In relating her story to Davis, Molly said that Lissy had told her that he wanted the strangulation to look like it was robbery and/or rape motivated so that it would throw the police off track and send them in the wrong direction. She said that Lissy had told her that he would be willing to pay her money if she could find someone who would be willing to do the job. He had figured that Molly would know someone like that, someone who would kill for money, because she was a street girl and hung out with people who would do almost anything for the right amount of cash. He knew, too, she said, that some of these people wouldn't require much money to do the job. Molly said that she had candidly acknowledged to Lissy that she might know several people like he wanted to hire.

At first Molly had thought that it was all a lot of bullshit, for which Lissy was known, and that it wouldn't go anywhere. But after reading about his wife's murder in the newspaper she realized that he hadn't been joking, at least not this time.

When Davis asked Molly how she had first met Lissy, she explained that it was through another girl, a prostitute who told her that Lissy was okay and that he paid well for "tricks." Early in March 1984, the prostitute had told Molly to go down to the corner of First Avenue and Yamhill Street in downtown Portland, and that Lissy would pick her up. After that first meeting, Lissy met with Molly several times a week between March and June.

"Usually he would drive around the block of Third and Fourth Avenues between Yamhill and Taylor Streets and signal me, after which I would walk down to First and Yamhill." That, she said, was Lissy's way to avoid detection by the police, who patrolled the downtown area heavily for johns. During their dates, they would usually drive up to an area of Washington Park behind the zoo, in Portland's affluent west hills, and park along a road that runs between the park and the zoo.

It was during the middle of June, Molly said, that Lissy had asked her to make the intimidating telephone calls to the mystery woman. At that same time he had also talked of getting a man beat up, and asked her to find a hit man for him.

"He mentioned three specific hits that he wanted done: a young woman, who he wanted strangled and possibly raped . . . he said she would think that she was being involved in a drug deal and that he would have her at a set place; a young man, who he wanted beaten within an inch of his life or killed; and an old couple on the coast, who he wanted to have an accident." Unfortunately, Molly didn't know the identities of any of the people Lissy had mentioned.

"Did he tell you when the killing would occur?"

"He said, 'Soon.' "

"Did he ever tell you why he wanted to have the woman killed?" Davis asked.

"No, he did not. . . . He asked me to find a hit man, told me that he would pay me to find a hit man."

"Did he tell you how much he would pay you?"

"A thousand dollars. . . . The young man, he said, was worth one hundred dollars to have beat up, and the other thing that I recall is that he said that he could provide a hit man with forty thousand dollars a year for doing hits for him and business associates of his . . . he also talked to me about an arson of a quarter-block warehouse."

"Did he say which warehouse?"

"He didn't say. Just a quarter-block-sized warehouse."

"Did you tell Lissy that you would look for a hit man for him?"

"No, I did not." Molly explained that she later had discussed with her boyfriend what Lissy had asked her to do for him, and her boyfriend had forbidden her to go near him again.

At the time Molly came forward with her story, Davis and Poppe didn't have much else to go on and were, in fact, on the wrong track, just as Lissy had planned if what Molly had told them was accurate. Although gut feelings kept telling the detectives that Lissy was somehow involved in Kathy's death, they didn't know who the actual killer was and didn't even have a clue as to who it *might* be. And Molly's statements, alone, weren't enough. She had seemed sincere and truthful enough, but they couldn't be certain of her motivations for coming forward with the story. Davis and Poppe knew that they had to get more evidence of Lissy's involvement if they were going to be able to build a case against him.

Six

It was 6:10 P.M. on Tuesday, July 10, when Detectives Lloyd Davis and David Poppe arrived at Michael Lissy's condominium in Lake Oswego after again making the two-hour drive from Eugene. It would mark their third contact with the victim's husband, who they both agreed was fast becoming a more viable suspect in Kathy's murder with each passing day. Lissy met them at the door, and informed them that Kathy's two sisters and parents were inside the residence. After exchanging greetings with Kathy's relatives, Lissy ushered the two detectives, at their request, back to the den where they could again talk privately with him.

Even though they had asked him previously, the two detectives again wanted to know when Lissy had first become aware of Kathy's business trip to Eugene. It was through the repetition of questions and answers that inconsistencies in a suspect's statements sometimes occurred, a common technique used by police. They had more than enough reasons to look for inconsistencies in Lissy's statements and to place him as a higher priority suspect: They had received the unsettling telephone call from Molly Griggs, and a search of Kathy's belongings found in Room 305 had turned up a partially used tube of toothpaste inside a cosmetics purse that had been packed inside a larger overnight bag. The toothpaste was the very item that Lissy had previously told them that Kathy had forgotten to take with her and had called home about. It was such an unacceptable excuse for anyone to call home about. And after *finding* the toothpaste they considered it an outright lie that Lissy had told them.

Lissy replied that he had first learned of Kathy's planned business trip to Eugene on Monday or Tuesday of the week she left, around July second or third. He said that she hadn't been particularly anxious about making the trip, but was nonetheless very happy because she had just been promoted at the bank and the trip was in part related to the promotion.

When they asked him again about Kathy's cocaine connection in Eugene, Lissy replied that the only name he could think of was Leslie Baker*, one of Kathy's "coke-snorting buddies from college." He added that Leslie had accompanied Kathy on one business trip to Eugene, and suggested that Kathy could have met her coke connection through Leslie. According to Lissy's statement, Kathy's use of cocaine could become quite heavy whenever Leslie was around. Leslie, he said, had often brought out Kathy's wild side.

As they had done on their first in-person meeting with Lissy, the detectives asked him to provide them with a rundown of his whereabouts on the fifth and sixth of July. Again, they were looking for inconsistencies in his statements, lies, in other words, as well as attempting to bring any new information to the surface that might have been previously omitted or overlooked. Lissy calmly explained that he had gone to work at 9:45 A.M. on July 5 at the Valley II store on Barbur Boulevard. He said that he probably went to the Valley I store in Northeast Portland at 11 A.M., and then likely went downtown at 11:30 A.M. to meet his ex-wife Elise for lunch. He said it was part of his usual routine to have lunch with her on Thursdays. The rest of the day was spent traveling back and forth between the two stores until, at 5:30 or 6 P.M., he and Roy Graham went to Walter Mitty's for drinks and hors d'oeuvres. He said that he had left Roy sometime between 8 and 8:30 P.M., and from Walter Mitty's had gone to Al Blackman's home and had accompanied Al to fix a flat tire. After fixing the flat tire he and Al had gone to a Häagen-Dazs ice cream parlor, ate some ice cream, and then returned to the Blackman residence. After dropping Al off, Lissy said he had gone on home, returned a previous call to his parents who resided on the Oregon coast, and then went to bed.

Hadn't he said earlier that he'd gone home from Walter Mitty's and *passed out*? He had made no mention during the previous interviews of fixing a tire with his friend, nor had he mentioned going out for ice cream and returning a telephone call to his parents on the coast. It seemed like a lot of activity to be involved in for someone who was on the verge of passing out, but the detectives kept their thoughts to themselves for the time being.

On July 6, the day Kathy's body was found, Lissy said he went to work at his usual time, 9:45 A.M. He said that he had planned to take his van to an upholstery shop to get the seats repaired, but couldn't remember whether he had done so or not on that particular day. Lissy said that he did recall that he had gone to a Print-Right shop in nearby Tigard where he had some sale flyers printed on bright red paper, one of which he used for a display ad in the newspaper. He had again seen his ex-wife Elise, who did his bookkeeping for him, and he had picked up his accounts receivables from her. Afterward he had kept an early afternoon appointment with a chiropractor. He had spent the remainder of the afternoon between the two stores, and at approximately 4:30 or 5 P.M. had met with Blackman to go to Walter Mitty's again for a drink. While at Walter Mitty's, he said, he had received a telephone call on his phone pager.

The phone call, he explained, had been from Sergeant Cline, but he hadn't been able to clearly understand the message on the voice pager. Since the message hadn't been clear to him, he drove to one of his stores where one of the employees told him to call the Eugene Police Department.

Seemingly out of the blue, Lissy changed the subject and brought up "Phil" again. He told the detectives that Phil was an ex-boyfriend of Kathy's who, after Lissy and Kathy had become engaged, had become upset and began professing his love for Kathy. The statement didn't seem to lead anywhere, except that perhaps Lissy was now trying to make a subtle attempt to bring Phil in as a suspect in Kathy's murder.

When they asked him why he had ordered that Kathy's body be cremated, Lissy said that he had done so because of an idea that both he and Kathy had felt that an open casket funeral was barbaric. He recalled having gone to his grandfather's funeral several years earlier, and remembered that his grandfather's corpse had looked chalky and waxen. He said that the memory of his grandfather's funeral had remained with him for a long time, and that he still couldn't get the sight out of his mind. He intimated that he didn't want to have that type of memory of Kathy. Asked about the ashes, Lissy said they were to be taken to the Hood Canal in Washington and scattered into the water. He said the location was significant because he and Kathy had once visited the Hood Canal and had enjoyed it very much. Kathy, he said, would have wanted her ashes distributed there.

Making no mention that they had heard that

Lissy had graduated from Harvard and Oxford, the detectives asked him about his education. Without hesitation Lissy responded that he had only a high-school education, and stated that he had graduated from a high school in Bremerton, Washington, near Tacoma.

Turning the conversation back to boyfriends Kathy may have had, Lissy brought out a photo and pointed out a man he identified as Fred Rice*. He added that he didn't know if Fred was the person he had previously named as "Jay," but insinuated that he might have been someone that she had seen or planned to see while in Eugene.

The person he knew as Jay, Lissy said, likely would have been a banking professional or perhaps a CPA, or someone closely aligned to Kathy's type of work. Although Lissy alleged that Kathy had had an affair with Jay, whoever he was, he stressed that he and Kathy had never discussed their extramarital affairs with each other. The only men he could recall Kathy telling him about was Jay and another man known to him only as Kirk.

Kirk, said Lissy, was an attorney from a small town on the Oregon coast. He said that Kathy and Kirk had been having an affair, which they had broken off approximately a month earlier, around the first part of June. As a result of the affair, Kathy and Lissy began counseling in an attempt to work out their marital problems.

"The counseling helped us to talk to each other rather than at each other," Lissy said.

Lissy added that another reason for their marital problems was his dramatic weight gain, which had damaged their sex life together. In an attempt to become more attractive to Kathy, Lissy said that he had begun dieting and had reduced his size from a triple-X to a single-X shirt, and had gone from a size forty-eight waist to a size forty-two pair of trousers. He explained that financial difficulties in his business had also created a problem in their marriage.

"Kathy told me on one occasion that I could make more money working at McDonald's than from running the scuba shops," Lissy said. "But I refused to quit." He said that he had felt that the answer to their financial problems was for him to continue running the shops.

"What about life insurance on Kathy?" Davis asked.

"There's some through the bank," Lissy said. "But I'm not aware of the amount or anything." Lissy explained that the president of the bank branch where Kathy had worked had told him there was some insurance, and Kathy Kolstad, a friend of Kathy's from the Network of Business and Professional Women of Portland, had told him that she was trying to determine if there was insurance coverage for the condominium.

At times during the interview Lissy seemed to become detached, as if his mind was beginning to wander, and he would change the subject and sometimes go off on a tangent of sorts. On one such digression he began recalling how, at Kathy's funeral, he had kept thinking about how he wasn't there, at the Valley River Inn, when Kathy was killed.

"It couldn't have been a stranger who got into the room," he said. "She wouldn't let a stranger in."

"Why did she use the Valley River Inn?" Poppe asked.

"She liked it, and she felt safe there."

"Do you remember when you first became aware of contracting VD?" Davis asked, changing the subject.

"About a week, maybe a week and a half ago." Lissy added that both he and Kathy had been treated by a doctor, and that it hadn't been the first time that he had contracted a venereal disease. They had also had a case of gonorrhea shortly after they first started living together.

"Do you think you got the VD from Kathy?" Davis asked.

"No. I think I brought it in." Lissy said that he might have contracted it from one of the street girls he had been having sex with. He said that he had been having a great deal of extra-curricular sex with many street girls, mostly oral sex. Until recently he had believed, mistakenly, that venereal diseases could not be contracted through oral sex.

"Is it possible that Kathy might have been in

debt to a dealer because of her coke habit?" Davis asked.

"No, I don't think so," Lissy said. "She mostly used coke from her job pressures, more of a spurty thing she did." Lissy said that Kathy had used cocaine mostly when she made her cold contacts with potential new clients. However, after getting the promotion, she had not been required to make cold contacts anymore and as a result had not used nearly as much cocaine as before. Lissy went on to explain that Kathy hadn't used cocaine around any of her friends at work or around any of her Network friends. She only used cocaine around her nonbusiness-type friends, according to Lissy.

Lissy suggested to the detectives that they contact an old boyfriend of Kathy's from college for more information about Kathy. The man's name was Melvin, but he didn't know his last name.

"Kathy's parents probably have that information," Lissy suggested.

At that point Davis excused himself to go and speak to Kathy's parents, leaving Lissy and Poppe alone in the den. Nothing was said between them for several minutes, until Lissy abruptly said: "I know I am a suspect."

"Yes," Poppe said. "Everybody is a suspect at this point. We're scratching for information." Poppe asked Lissy if he had intended to go to Eugene with Kathy for the business trip.

"She asked me to go on Wednesday night, the night before she left," Lissy said. He explained that he had been unable to go because of having to place some advertisements in the newspaper for a sale he was planning for Friday, July 13, at the scuba shops.

Fifteen minutes later Davis came back into the room, and Poppe rose from the sofa to leave.

"Melvin's name is Reese," Davis said. "Melvin Reese*. Kathy's parents told me that he now lives in Houston, Texas."

Seven

Kathryn Ann Martini-Lissy's murder was an unusual story, and was fast becoming a big story. Those closest to the case acknowledged that her death wasn't the typical murder where a woman was strangled and left naked near the side of a road after hitchhiking; in other words, her death wasn't directly the result of her own actions or lifestyle like so many other homicides. Her death was different, making for a different kind of story. It began making big news as much because of the upstanding type of woman that Kathy had been in the community as it had because of the mysterious circumstances surrounding her death. All of the newspapers in the Eugene-Springfield area carried the story, as well as those throughout the Willamette Valley. Even *The Oregonian* in Portland (the largest newspaper in the state) reported it because of Kathy's connection to and high standing in that city's banking community. She had never made that paper's high-society page, but they were sure interested in her now. Murder made sensational headlines, and sensational headlines sold newspapers. Stories ran in the paper right after her body had been found, and continued for several days. Additional stories ran after the medical examiner's office reported that her death was the result of strangulation that possibly had been motivated by rape or some other type of sexual assault. Although it hadn't been any of the newspapers' intentions, it was nonetheless a direct result of the news stories that Molly Griggs had become an integral part of the investigation and had ultimately helped Detectives Lloyd Davis and David Poppe begin to unravel the intricate web of lies and deception that had been so carefully spun by others.

Shortly after their initial contact with Molly, Davis and Poppe spoke with Officer David Houck, a policeman with the Portland Police Bureau, who confirmed what Molly had told Davis and Poppe about Lissy frequenting the area of Southwest Fourth Avenue and Taylor Street where, according to Molly, Lissy and Molly had repeatedly engaged in fellatio for a fee. Officer Houck told the detectives that he knew Michael Lissy and that during May 1984 he had seen him in the aforementioned area on three or four occasions. On one of those occasions, Houck said, Lissy had told him that he was having financial problems and was very near having to file for bankruptcy.

Molly, meanwhile, reiterated what Lissy had told her in June about wanting several people killed and another person severely beaten. Lissy had said that he wanted the young man beaten because he was somehow "fucking up the money flow," and had said that he wanted an older couple killed because they were standing in the way of some sort of development that Lissy was supposedly involved in. Lissy had suggested to Molly that the older couple could be killed in a way that would appear to be an accident, like having them fall down a long flight of stairs or having them pushed off a boat. This was all in addition, of course, to having the "young woman" raped and strangled.

The scenario that involved Molly broadened and intensified soon after Davis and Poppe obtained a court order for her to wear a body wire, a transmitting device that sends out voice transmission signals that can be received and recorded by police using special receiving equipment tuned to a particular frequency. The plan was to have Molly talk to Lissy while wearing the body wire whereby he would, they hoped, make incriminating admissions of his involvement in or responsibility for his wife's murder. However, when Molly called Lissy the first time, the plan went awry when he refused to meet with her in person. Davis and Poppe didn't know quite what to make of it. They thought that perhaps he had been alarmed by their visit to him on July 10 and had been "spooked" by their questions, or perhaps he had suddenly become paranoid.

Even though Lissy wouldn't meet with Molly on the first attempt, Davis and Poppe didn't give

up. They checked Molly into a room at the Portland Motor Hotel—where they would keep her
"safe" from Lissy for the next several days—
downtown near the location where she had met
Lissy on prior occasions. Using telephone wiretap equipment, they had Molly continue calling
him. Finally, on the third such attempt, Lissy
agreed to meet her at noon on July 12, at Portland's downtown Yamhill Market, a multilevel
galleria of stores and restaurants that encom-
passes an entire city block.

Molly waited patiently. She walked around the
market, stopped at shops and looked at greeting
cards until, finally, she saw Lissy drive by in a
maroon Datsun 300 Z. He appeared to glance
in her direction, but did not stop. For some reason—perhaps he sensed the police surveillance—
Lissy did not return. Molly returned to her hotel
room and called Lissy again. She arranged a second meeting at the same location for 2 P.M. that
same day, but that time Lissy didn't show up at
all.

Despite the failed attempts to lure Lissy into a
meeting with Molly, the cops didn't want to give
up. They instructed Molly to call him again. But
he was reluctant to meet her anywhere until she
said: "This sounded just like the plot you described to me when you wanted to have someone
killed. I am worried that I am involved and want
you to help me get away because the police will
be contacting me. I need some money to get out
of town." Wanting to hush her up, he finally

agreed to meet her at a downtown Denny's, located at Southwest Fourth Avenue and Lincoln Street, at 9:30 P.M. on July 12.

Molly arrived by taxi about five minutes early, at 9:25 P.M. With the police surveillance team already in position and out of sight, Molly walked across the parking lot and headed toward the restaurant's entrance.

"Molly," someone yelled as she reached for the door. She turned, and saw Lissy sitting on a low cement wall several yards away in an area obscured by bushes. She walked toward him. "Let's go somewhere," he said, motioning toward his blue van parked nearby.

"No, let's go inside, get a cup of coffee," Molly said, fearful for her life. She momentarily recalled how, after Lissy had asked her to help him find a hit man, her boyfriend had warned her to stay away from him. She also recalled how he had come downtown in his van a few times after having made the request for her to find him a hit man and would follow her. She didn't know precisely how many times he had actually followed her and watched her from a distance, but on the occasions that she had seen him, she always turned and walked the other way because she was scared of him. But sometimes he would park his van, get out, and try to follow her on foot, which had frightened her even more. Now she was meeting with him after his wife had been murdered, and she was terrified. He kept pushing her to get inside his van so that they could "go somewhere," but Molly insisted that they go inside for coffee. Eventually, Lissy reluctantly agreed. After being seated at a booth and receiving their coffee, Molly began talking about Kathy's murder and the fact that she had heard that she might have been raped.

"I think my phone's tapped," he said. "That's why I didn't want you talking about the murder over the phone." Lissy, of course, was only guessing. He didn't know for certain that Davis and Poppe had applied for and received a court order to have a device installed by Pacific Northwest Bell Telephone Company that would register all numbers dialed from Lissy's home telephone number. But he suspected it, and was being very careful who he called.

"How do you know it's tapped?"

"I can hear little clicking sounds. It's tapped, I'm almost certain of it."

"I believe you had your wife killed," Molly said.

"I loved Kathy," he said. "I'm really fucking upset about it. She was strangled and raped."

Molly reminded Lissy that he had told her that the woman he wanted killed would be strangled and raped, but he didn't take the bait. He sat quietly instead and did not respond.

"Did you bring the money so I can get out of town?" Molly asked.

"No. We have to go to the bank and get it." He explained that he had to withdraw the money from an automatic teller machine.

"I'll wait here," Molly insisted.

"I'll be back in about two-and-a-half minutes," Lissy said when he realized that Molly wouldn't go anywhere with him. But he didn't give up easily. "Why don't you go to the Red Lion next door and meet me there?" The Red Lion was a hotel located adjacent to Denny's, but Molly didn't want to risk crossing the dark parking lot to comply with his wishes. She was afraid that she might not be in sight of the police at some point, and that he might meet her in the shadows and drag her into his van.

"No, I'll wait for you here," Molly said. Lissy didn't persist any longer. He got up from their table and walked quickly out of the restaurant. After Lissy left, Molly got up and waited inside the entrance area of the restaurant. A few minutes later she saw Lissy's van pull up in the taxi zone on Lincoln Street, at which point she walked outside.

Lissy rolled down the window of his van and held a wad of bills just below the window line so that it couldn't be seen from the outside by anyone who might be watching. She grabbed it, put it inside her purse, and climbed into a cab that she had instructed to be waiting nearby. She told the cabbie to drive her to the Hilton Hotel, located downtown on Broadway and Salmon Street, where she was met inside the lobby by Detective Edward Van Horn of the Eugene Police Department. To evade Lissy in case he was watching, Van Horn quickly ushered Molly out of an exit on the opposite side of the hotel from where she had entered and drove her back to her "safe" room at the Portland Motor Hotel a few blocks away.

Once inside the hotel room, Van Horn took pictures of the money—$300—first while it was still inside Molly's purse and then again as another detective placed it inside an evidence envelope. Molly was subsequently paid $750 by the Eugene Police Department for her efforts through negotiations with her attorney, and she moved to a location where she hoped Lissy wouldn't be able to find her.

Interestingly, the money Lissy had given Molly consisted of a number of $50 bills, which was strange if he had just withdrawn it from an automatic teller machine, like he had said. Automatic teller machines in Portland only dispensed $5 and $20 bills, not fifties. He must have had the money with him all the time, the cops reasoned. So why had he tried so hard to coax Molly into going with him to the bank? The implication was chilling, and Molly Griggs was grateful to be out of his reach. She only hoped that she could remain out of his reach until the whole sordid affair was over and Lissy was behind bars.

Eight

On July 13, 1984, at 8:53 A.M., Detectives Lloyd Davis and David Poppe called Michael Lissy's phone number, in Lake Oswego, from their office in Eugene. After turning on the telephone recording equipment authorized by a court order, Poppe stated the purpose, date, and time for the call. They were following up on the previous evening's activities involving Molly Griggs and Lissy, and, still employing techniques to find inconsistencies in their prime suspect's statements, hoped to gain Lissy's confidence and bring his deception closer to the surface.

"Hello," Lissy said, promptly answering the phone.

"Hello," Detective David Poppe said. "May I please speak with Mike Lissy?"

"This is he."

"Mike, this is Detective Poppe calling from Eugene."

"Yes."

"How are you doing?"

"Okay." There was no background noise, only silence until one of them spoke.

"Mike Cline told us that he got a call from you yesterday. He tried to call you back, but I understand he talked with your attorney?"

"Okay."

"About some calls you've been getting?"

"Yeah." Lissy appeared as if he was being careful, and wasn't going to volunteer any information to the detectives. He was going to make them ask for it.

"Can you tell us about that?"

"Well, I've had a couple of crank calls." Lissy paused for a moment, then spoke slowly, as if finding his way and searching for the right words.

"I hope I didn't call you at a bad time." Poppe, of course, knew that anytime was a bad time for Lissy to get a call from a couple of cops investigating his wife's murder, especially when he knew that they were now looking at him as the perpetrator.

"No, no," Lissy said, lying. "In one of the calls the caller said, 'Your wife must have been a bad lay for him to have killed her,' and then just hung up. The other one was a gal, a hooker that I'd gone out with that said, 'You are involved, and if you don't give me some money, I'm gonna go to the police.' "

"She's blackmailing you?"

"It looks like it. When she called the second time I just gave her my attorney's number and hung up."

"That's pretty good," said Poppe. Davis quickly cut in:

"This is Davis on the other line. Did she happen to call your attorney or did he ever say?"

"He didn't say. I would be real, real surprised if she did."

"Okay. When was the last time she called you, Mike?" Davis asked.

"Umm, uh, yesterday." That much was the truth, but it had been difficult for him to spit it out.

"Yesterday? Uh-huh. Was that the same attorney that Poppe and Cline talked to? Michael Sturgeon?"

"Yeah. I'm just referring everything to him. There's people calling about estate planning." He laughed nervously.

"Jesus. That's unbelievable," Davis said.

"I know." Lissy paused, and sounded like he was trying to control his emotions. "I'm sorry. It's just I can't believe all the vultures that come out."

"Yeah. What a society we've got here," Davis said.

"Who is this person that's blackmailing you? Do you know her name?" Poppe asked.

"Her name is Holly." Lissy's voice was clear and deliberate now.

"Holly? Is that with an 'H,' as in Hal?" Davis asked. Davis had to be sure. He wanted the deception clearly documented on the tape.

"Yeah, uh-huh. But it's probably not her real

name. I didn't really recognize the voice and I can't put a face with it. She wanted me to meet her at the Yamhill Market and I started to go down there, and then I thought, 'No, I don't want to get involved in anything like that.' So I went over and talked to my attorney and he said to just refer anything like that to him."

"Did she say anything when you said that she should talk to your attorney if she wanted to talk to you further?" Poppe asked.

"No. I just said, 'Goodbye,' and hung up."

"Did you tell her that, about contacting your attorney? Did I understand you correctly?" Poppe asked.

"Yeah. I just told her to call my attorney, Michael Sturgeon, and said 'Goodbye,' and hung up."

"You said she called you a couple of times," Davis said. "Is that two or three, or what, Mike?"

"Two." A lie. Molly had called him at least twice that many times.

"Two times?"

"Yeah."

"Did she ever demand any money?" Davis asked.

"She said she was scared, and wanted some money."

"Why in the heck would she say that?" Davis asked. "I mean, what's the deal with her? Do you understand that, Mike?"

"I assume, you know, that she's just trying to shake some money out of me."

"You said you used her as a prostitute. How many times approximately?" Davis asked.

"If it's who I think it is, probably three, four times. And I would assume that they're figurin' because I went to prostitutes that I didn't, uh, love my wife or somethin'," Lissy said.

"Um-huh." *What a scumbag*, reflected the detectives to themselves.

"That's all I can figure," Lissy said.

"It's got me kind of confused how she figures she's going to get any money out of you other than by besmirching your reputation or something," Davis said.

"Well, that could be, you know. The first time she called, it just shook the hell out of me."

"Mike, I know it's difficult to remember. But do you remember when the first time was she called, approximately? The date and the time?" Poppe asked.

"Day before last," Lissy said after hesitating for several moments.

"Day before yesterday?" Davis asked. That was the day they had visited him in Lake Oswego, but Davis didn't bring it up. He knew that Molly had called him for the first time on the twelfth, only a day ago, and that the money transaction between Molly and Lissy had occurred on the evening of the twelfth.

"Yeah."

"Two days ago, say the eleventh. Roughly what time?" Davis asked, playing along.

"In the evening."

"That was the time she said she was scared? Correct me if I'm wrong," Poppe said.

"She said she wanted the money, to get out of town. But I felt it was a shakedown, and I just sort of let it go. Then when the second call came—"

Davis cut him off.

"Let's back up to the first one, Mike," Davis said. "Do you remember what you told her? I know it's difficult."

"I just said, well, 'we have to get together and talk,' or something. And she said, 'Well, let's meet at the Yamhill Market.' I started to go down and then didn't, and she called back all irate."

"Well, when did she call back, Mike?" Davis asked.

"Oh, five or six or seven, last night."

"Last night?"

"Yeah. It was after I had gone to talk to Sturgeon."

"Mike, I've been writing notes here, trying to keep up here," Poppe said. "And as usual, when you write something you miss some other things. The first call was two days ago in the evening."

"Yeah."

"And she wanted money at that time?"

"Yeah."

"What did she say she'd do if you didn't give it to her?" Poppe said.

"She said she'd go to the police. Well, she

really didn't say that, it was just the impression I got."

"Well, what did she say to give you that impression, Mike?" Davis asked.

"She just said, 'I have a lot of information that could hurt you,' or. . . ." He trailed off.

"Trying to scare you or something?" Davis asked.

"It wasn't really anything directly that she said. It was just the impression I got."

"I'm trying to remember back to that time," Poppe said. "The days start drawing together when you work too long. But I remember when we talked last you told us about using a prostitute on occasion."

"Right."

"I guess what has confused me, is, why didn't you just tell her that the police already know all about it, or something like that?" Poppe asked.

"Just, you know, I don't know," Lissy said, grasping for words. "I was just afraid that it was going to come out in the public. Just spooked me, you know, I think, because of the fact that she had my home phone number. I never gave that out."

"You mean to the prostitutes?" Davis asked.

"Yeah."

"Do you know how she got it?"

"No. But with all the publicity, she could look it up in the phone book. We do have a listed phone number."

"Okay. How's that listed?" Davis asked.

"It's, uh, I don't even know. That's how Sturgeon looked me up one time. I told him that I didn't know how she got my phone number, and he said it was in the phone book."

"We get a lot of harassing phone call complaints, believe me," Poppe said. "And this is pretty damn bad when they're bothering you at this time. But what we recommend is that you start keeping a log. Put a pad and pencil right by the phone. I hope you don't get any more, but if you do you can keep an accurate log of when you got it and what was said. Also, like you already said, you can refer people to your attorney. You might consider changing your number, too."

"I've been thinking that." He wandered off for a moment, then began to ramble. "It may sound strange, but sharing the grief with a friend seems to, you know, it relieves . . . people around the country are slowly but surely getting the word, you know, because there's no real master list to call . . . you know, I'm torn. The one phone call just . . . God, I can't believe anybody could be that gross and cruel."

"That first call you talked about?" Poppe asked.

"Yeah. I mean, Jesus." Lissy sounded as if he might begin to cry.

"Just to regress a second here, you said you got another call, last night?" Davis asked, trying to put the conversation back on track. "Same girl? Same hooker?"

"I guess. It sure sounded the same."

"Sounded the same, huh?"

"Yeah. Sturgeon just said to refer 'em to him and then hang up."

"Do you remember anything she said on the second one?" Davis asked.

"She said, 'Well, you didn't make the appointment, and you really let me down,' et cetera, et cetera."

"And you told her just to call Sturgeon?" Davis asked.

"Yeah."

"What did she think of that?"

"Nothing. Because I just said, 'Goodbye,' and hung up."

"Oh. That's pretty good advice, telling her to call your attorney," Poppe said.

"Yeah. The first time, I was in a state of shock, and then I panicked. God, you know, I don't want this coming out. It's not even so much me that I'm concerned about. I don't want Kathy, you know, dragged through the mud. I'm praying that the drugs and the extracurricular, uh . . ."

"Activities?"

"Yeah, activities, don't come out."

"One thing we used to advise people on dealing with harassing phone calls was to use a whistle and blow into the phone. But we found, over the years, that what they do is return the call and then blow a whistle back in your ear, and it'll almost take your head off. So I don't really suggest that," Davis said.

"I'm really thinking that on Monday I'm just gonna have the number switched."

"You can have the number switched," Davis said. "Or the minute they call, just like Dave says, take notes, date and time and that stuff." Davis and Poppe were playing along with Lissy, of course, as a means to build his trust or confidence in them and, they hoped, throw off his suspicions about his phone being tapped.

"It's possible," Poppe cut in, "and I don't know what you think, but if, for example, there's any possibility that one of these people is connected with what happened to Kathy, uh, we'd like to get any information that might be valuable."

"Yeah."

"We're doing a lot down here, now," Davis said. "And there's enough information and leads to keep ten people busy."

"Another thing, if you could figure out who that girl is, Michael, it would sure help us because we'd like to go talk to her," Poppe said. "She might have something. Maybe she's not out just to hassle you. So if you can figure out who she is, we'd like to go talk to her." He felt like laughing, but managed to maintain his professionalism and self-control.

"The thing is," Lissy said, "that I don't really recognize the voice. I never really paid much attention to names. But I'll think on it as hard as I can."

"Okay. If you can come up with anything that will help us do our follow-up, we'd appreciate it," Poppe said.

"She's usually out in the evening," Lissy said. "Maybe I can get somebody to go with me and I can go out and see if I can find her."

"We don't know who did it down here," Poppe said. "We're talkin' to the nuts in town as well to the businesspeople."

"Yeah, we don't want you going out and making our contacts," Davis said, cutting in again. "We've got to do the police work."

"When I even said that, I just feel so fucking guilty anyway, for, uh, well. . . ." Lissy said, trailing off again. It sounded like he had begun to cry.

"Don't blame yourself," Davis said. "We're not trying to get you . . . About the coke, we've talked to Leslie, but can you come up with anything on that cocaine connection down here? A name or anything?"

"No, uh, I bought her coke once, before the wedding," Lissy said.

"Oh, did you?" Davis asked.

"That was the only time, though."

"Was that up there in Portland or down here in Eugene?"

"That was up here."

"Was it someone she would know?"

"No, it was actually just a friend. Before the

wedding, she didn't have time to go to Eugene
and she wanted some because Leslie was coming
out here. But she knew I didn't really do it, and
because of the tight finances. . . ." He indicated
that he really couldn't afford to buy it at the
time.

"And the wedding probably cost a pretty
penny," Poppe said.

"Well, her dad picked up a pretty good por-
tion of that."

"Okay, another thing. What about Jay?" Poppe
asked. "We haven't been able to come up with
anything about Jay."

"You know, Jay might be Fred."

"Oh, that might be Fred," Poppe said.

"That's right. You mentioned that the other
day when we were up there," Davis said.

"My remembrance of names, well . . . Kathy
and I had an agreement that we didn't talk
about, you know. . . ."

"Your extracurricular activities," Poppe said,
finishing the statement for Lissy.

"Yeah. So, the only one I knew much about
was the one from the coast. And that was only
because we each focused on one last relationship
and why we should end things . . . I'm getting
disoriented again . . . so believe me, I just keep
going over in my mind about everything, and it
just frustrates me because all I can do is come
up with blanks for Eugene. Like, say, Jay may
be Fred. It may not be. I don't think she'd had
any contact with Fred in, you know, a year or a

year and a half. And I know she was seeing somebody down there."

"And Jay was just a name that kept coming to your mind, huh?" Poppe asked.

"Yeah. I don't even know a den there where she got her coke from. I always just assumed that it was a guy she was getting it from. But she could have been getting it from a woman. She wouldn't have been involved in the street scene there. She would have had to have gotten it from one of her friends there, you know, who had a connection. She just wouldn't have been out in the street scene at all. That just wasn't Kathy."

"Mike, if you happen to change your number, could you let us know please?" Poppe asked.

"Sure."

"Okay. And please contact us if you hear anything at all, or if you think of anything that we can use."

"Okay."

"Take care, Mike. We'll be seein' you."

"Okay."

There was no longer any doubt in their minds that Lissy was being dishonest with them. Lissy knew Molly Griggs, and he knew that her name wasn't "Holly." He had just said that he really didn't know the person who had begun calling him, and it was obvious that he had tried to lead the detectives to a different, fictitious person. The fact was, they knew that Lissy had met with Molly twenty or more times. She had told them so, and because she had come to them in the first place with information about Lissy's possible involvement in Kathy's murder they had no reason to doubt her. Yet Lissy insisted that he didn't know her name, and never did he mention that he had paid her $300 on the previous evening to get her out of town. Lissy was lying to them, and it was becoming increasingly clearer to Davis and Poppe that he was taking steps to throw them off the trail of Kathy's killer because he knew it would eventually lead them straight to him.

Nine

In conducting their follow-up probe into Kathy's murder, Detectives Lloyd Davis and David Poppe contacted Clark Miller, executive vice president of the Bank of Boston. Miller went through Kathy's employment history for the detectives, and told them that she had life insurance worth approximately $37,000. However, he said, the insurance policy had a multiplier clause attached to it. If she was killed while traveling on business for the bank the insurance would be worth nearly $200,000. Miller, reading from a file folder, told the detectives that Michael Lissy had been named as the beneficiary of her insurance on November 7, 1983, before they were even married. In fact, Lissy had not yet obtained the divorce from Elise, who had been either his third or fourth wife; the detectives still weren't sure which.

Davis and Poppe looked at each other quizzically regarding Miller's information. The insurance was enough, they silently agreed, to motivate Lissy to either murder Kathy himself or to have her murdered. Many people, the detectives knew,

had been killed for a lot less money in insurance
and murder-for-hire schemes. And the insurance
on Kathy's life was just a part of it. There was
mortgage insurance to consider on the condo, as
well as all the other material possessions that they
had accumulated and that Kathy had brought
into the marriage, all of which Lissy stood to in-
herit from Kathy's estate.

Michael David Lissy was born Michael David
Reid on March 18, 1949, in San Diego, California, to Wallace and Patricia Reid. Lissy, the detectives learned, had changed his name when
his mother divorced his natural father and married Ernest Lissy, who had officially adopted
him. Strangely, the name change occurred after
"Michael Reid" had already reached adulthood,
while the family was living in Seattle, Washington.

At one point during their background probe
on Lissy, Davis and Poppe discovered that Lissy
had experienced a number of burglaries and
robberies during the years of 1976, 1977, and
1981. They uncovered information which showed
that Lissy purportedly had been the victim of a
holdup at a North Portland Kentucky Fried
Chicken outlet where he had worked as an assistant manager. They also turned up information that he had reported being the victim of
two other armed robberies of his person. He had
also reported a March 23, 1977, burglary of his

apartment, located at 4228 Southeast Thirty-ninth Street in Portland, in which valuable antiques were taken, some $10,000 worth.

In the latest burglary that they had been able to turn up information about, the one that had occurred in 1981 shortly after his marriage to Elise and which Davis and Poppe chose to focus on because of the extensive investigation that had been conducted at the time, several expensive items had been taken from Lissy's apartment at 6828 N.E. Killingsworth Street. In that case he had filed a major insurance claim which was considered suspicious by the insurance carrier, Farmers Insurance Companies of Oregon. As a result, Farmers had ordered an investigation into the April 3, 1981, loss. When Davis and Poppe studied the case files related to the claim, they uncovered a wealth of information about Lissy, most of it unflattering though not particularly surprising. Among other things, the insurance investigators had written: "The insured appears to be intentionally concealing his employment status and past employment history for unknown reasons." The statement sufficiently piqued the detectives' interest enough that they were compelled to read on.

The insurance investigation revealed contact with Lissy's former supervisor, Ronald Nolan*, at the Kentucky Fried Chicken store. Nolan, who ultimately had fired Lissy for embezzlement of company money, recalled that Lissy always seemed to have a large amount of cash in his possession when he worked at the outlet. Although he had investigated Lissy's money-handling procedures at the store and discovered irregularities, he could not immediately document the deviations from proper company procedure that he suspected Lissy of making. Nonetheless, he felt that Lissy had been pocketing the money and continued to watch him closely.

According to Nolan's account, Lissy had worked for Circle K stores, a chain of convenience stores, prior to his employment with Kentucky Fried Chicken, and his references appeared to have been good. Lissy had been hired as an assistant manager of the North Lombard Street shop, and despite Nolan suspecting him of cash theft, was later promoted to manager of the North Killingsworth Street store because the higher-ups apparently liked him. Nolan said that he had formed the impression from talking with Lissy that Lissy and his stepfather, Ernest, were operating various business enterprises on the side and that they had extensive rental property holdings. But, he stressed, he could never tell when Lissy was telling the truth or lying. Nolan had suspected that the businesses had been held and operated only by Lissy's stepfather.

When the Kentucky Fried Chicken store was held up, supposedly at gunpoint, Nolan indicated that he had felt that the robbery was not genuine. A subsequent police investigation had come up blank, and Lissy had filed a worker's compensation insurance claim after the robbery. Nolan had told the investigators that he would not hire Lissy back under any circumstances.

Davis and Poppe noted that another of Lissy's former supervisors at Kentucky Fried Chicken, Tom Larson* had been extremely reluctant to discuss Lissy with the insurance investigators. Larson had told them that he and his wife were concerned that Lissy would find out that they had talked about him and attempt to harm them. Speaking slowly and carefully, Larson expressed fear that Lissy had the capability of directing physical harm toward him through others. Larson had eventually agreed to talk, but only if his identity was not revealed.

Larson had said that he tried to have Lissy "put in jail," because of what he had felt was a fraudulent robbery of the Lombard Street Kentucky Fried Chicken store. Lissy, the assistant manager, usually worked with Joe Hellmac*, the head cook and a personal friend of Lissy's. Prior to Lissy coming on board, the Lombard Street store had been the most profitable outlet in the Portland region. However, after Lissy began working there, extensive cash shortages began to crop up and the store plummeted in its rating. Larson tried to demonstrate to his supervisors that Lissy was embezzling money from the store, to no avail. Instead, Larson ended up taking the blame for many of the shortages.

On May 29, 1977, Larson arrived at the store in the early morning hours and found Lissy tied to the counter, the front door locked, the back door open, and $1,200 missing from the store's safe. Larson was adamant that the robbery had been faked by Lissy. Two weeks after the robbery, Larson sent Lissy out to purchase change for the store and noted, upon Lissy's return, that he brought back coins in wrappers that appeared to Larson to be identical to wrappers that contained the change that had been stolen in the robbery.

Soon after the robbery, Lissy began wearing a neck brace and filed a worker's compensation claim with the parent company's insurance carrier. Larson said that he instructed another employee to follow Lissy on occasion, particularly after work. The other worker reported that as soon as Lissy was out of sight of the store, he would take off the neck brace. After Lissy's promotion to manager and transfer to another store, Hellmac told Larson that Lissy had "ripped off the safe," on more than one occasion.

Larson stated that on one occasion Lissy told him that he had purchased a $50,000 double-indemnity life-insurance policy on his wife at the time, Francis "Frankie" Mae Schuster, and that Lissy was planning to arrange an accident for her so that he could collect the insurance money. In relating the plan that had been told to him, Larson had characterized Lissy as "insane," and noted that Lissy had told him that he owned a Rolls-Royce, an airplane, and various properties and businesses. Larson recalled a time in which

Lissy had discussed a burglary of his own home in which approximately $10,000 worth of antiques were stolen. Larson also said that Lissy had what he felt was an unusual interest in young women, and described him as a smooth talker who was able to convince most people of his credibility. Larson said he felt that Lissy made his living by "defrauding" people.

When Hellmac was contacted by the insurance investigators and was asked if he knew Michael Lissy, his initial response was that he had never heard of him. However, when confronted about having been the head cook at the Kentucky Fried Chicken outlet where Lissy had worked, he had become very excited and upset. When the investigators explained that they were investigating the burglary of Lissy's apartment and were interested in talking with Hellmac about Lissy's past employment and known associates, Hellmac became very belligerent.

He said that he was "not taking no shit," and that he had not seen that "son of a bitch" for two years.

"If Lissy's trying to lay some trip on me, then he is full of shit," Hellmac said. He stated that Lissy had caused him some trouble in the past, but when asked about it he said that it was "nothing anybody should know about." He said that Lissy was a "lying sack of shit," which he repeated several times. After a pause, he asked the investigators to not tell Lissy what he had said about him. He also said that he didn't believe the burglary they were investigating was genuine.

"He's pulled this shit before," he said, refusing to comment further about his statement. Hellmac expressed his dismay that the investigators had been able to locate him, and commented that Lissy was "going to pay for this one." He said that he had been living a "perfectly happy life" for three years without Lissy, and insisted that Lissy was "bullshitting" the investigators "up one side and down the other." He indicated that he knew information about some of Lissy's past activities.

Hellmac first met Lissy in 1976, when Lissy managed a Circle K convenience store at 176th Avenue and Division Street in Portland. Hellmac was eighteen at the time, and Lissy was approximately twenty-eight. Lissy hired him to work at the store, and shortly afterward the entire store crew was fired due to excessive cash and inventory shortages. At the time of everyone's firing, he and Lissy had moved in together and were sharing an apartment in East Portland.

Shortly after the firings, Lissy had obtained the job as assistant manager at the Kentucky Fried Chicken store by supplying false job application information and fraudulent references. Although Hellmac had obtained a job as a "shingle counter" after being fired from the Circle K store, he soon quit the job to go to work for Lissy at Kentucky Fried Chicken. According to his characterization of Lissy, Lissy was a "bullshitter" and a convincing "smooth talker." He said he was amazed at how easily and convincingly Lissy could lie and make up stories and schemes. Lissy was particularly effective with his lying when he was under pressure from his supervisor.

Hellmac, approximately six feet tall and weighing 180 pounds, had long, shoulder-length brown hair and was single when he and Lissy had lived together. He stated that Lissy had just obtained a divorce from a wife in Washington State, but did not know the former wife's name because Lissy had never discussed the details of his prior marriage with him. During the approximately one year that they lived together, Lissy had met a young girl named Virginia Meyer* who hung around with a girlfriend whom Hellmac knew only as Lori. He described the girls as approximately seventeen years old, and said the girls were together most of the time. Virginia was a "white, skinny, red-haired girl who liked black men," and Lissy and she had become close friends and had often engaged in sexual encounters inside the bathroom at the Kentucky Fried Chicken store. It was Hellmac's belief that Lissy had been paying Virginia for her sexual favors with either money or drugs.

At the Lombard Street store, Lissy had set up a "short ringing" system which allowed him to pocket a significant amount of cash on a daily basis. As a result, the store began running regular chicken inventory shortages for which the store manager, Tom Larson, was forced to take the blame from company executives. Lissy somehow had arranged the shortages so that they had always showed up on Larson's shifts.

At first Lissy was only taking approximately $100 per day, part of which he shared with the other employees who were involved in or knew about the scheme. But as he began to take more and more money, a problem with the chicken inventory arose and Lissy was forced to purchase cheaper and poorer quality whole chickens from a local poultry wholesaler. He would bring the chickens to the Lombard Street store, cut them up, and place them into the higher quality chicken inventory supplied by the parent company to make up for the shortages. At that point, according to Hellmac, Lissy was shorting the till by approximately $200 per day. He soon started a system in which he would cut the cash register tape, after taking in a certain amount of money, so that he would not have to ring up sales at all after reaching a certain point in the day's business. This practice went on for about six months.

In the early part of 1978, Lissy and Hellmac moved into a house at 6222 North Missouri Avenue, which was owned by Lissy's stepfather, Ernest. Shortly thereafter, in April 1978, Lissy married Frankie Schuster, whom he had met at the Lombard Street store. It was at approximately that same time that Lissy was promoted to manager of the Killingsworth Street store, located only a few blocks away from the Lombard Street store.

Lissy instructed Hellmac on how to continue the "short ringing" scheme at the Lombard Street store, and began the same system at the Killingsworth Street store. By that time, Hellmac estimated, Lissy was stealing more than $1,000 weekly between the two stores.

By mid-year 1978, Lissy had begun discussing with Hellmac and two other men, Larry Simpson* and Donald Moore*, both of whom had been hired in late 1977, a plan in which he would purchase a sailboat and smuggle narcotics into the United States. Lissy had originally planned to use the money he had been embezzling to buy the sailboat, but instead suddenly purchased a new car, a Monte Carlo. When the money was gone, Lissy began discussing plans in which his new wife, Frankie, would be murdered. He had taken out an insurance policy on her life, and had told Simpson and Hellmac that he wanted them to push her down a flight of stairs during a burglary he would set up. However, before the plan could be carried out, Frankie left Lissy, had the policy canceled, and filed for a divorce.

As the shortages continued at the Lombard Street store, Hellmac was forced to quit by early 1979 while Lissy was stealing larger and larger amounts from the Killingsworth Street store. During this same period Lissy began courting Elise Dunn, who was an employee of Lissy's at the Killingsworth Street store, all the while maintaining his sexual liaisons with Virginia. Lissy hired Hellmac, who had been unemployed for several months, as a janitor at the outlet he managed.

Then one night, still in the early part of 1979, while Lissy and Hellmac were working, supervisor and company executive Ronald Nolan showed up. He called Lissy into the back room and, after several minutes, reappeared and informed Hellmac that he had just fired Lissy. Although Nolan told him that he was welcome to remain on the job, Hellmac chose to quit on the spot.

A short time later he moved out of the house he had been sharing with Lissy on Missouri Street. Lissy subsequently married Elise Dunn and moved in with her at the apartment she already occupied on Killingsworth Street. Although his memory was vague, he recalled a discussion he'd had with Lissy in which Lissy talked about murdering Elise's mother so that he could obtain Elise's inheritance. Hellmac suggested that the investigators talk to Larry Simpson who, he said, could provide more details on the latest murder plot that Lissy had so callously engineered.

The next time Hellmac had seen Lissy was in mid-1980 when he observed Lissy delivering telephone books in Portland, assisted by Virginia. He told the insurance investigators that he was certain that Lissy, though again married, had been dating Virginia behind his new wife's back.

Although initially reluctant to discuss the May 27, 1979, robbery of the Lombard Street Kentucky Fried Chicken restaurant, Hellmac had finally agreed to tell the investigators what happened when he realized they weren't out to get him for the crime. After he and Lissy were fired from the Circle K store and Lissy subsequently had gone to work at the Lombard Street Kentucky Fried Chicken restaurant, Lissy had indicated that he wanted some "fast cash." He had not yet begun his "shortchanging" system, and instructed Hellmac to appear at the store at 11 P.M., after closing, and to wear a white shirt so that he'd look like an employee.

When he arrived, Lissy gave him approximately $1,500, the entire day's receipts, and had him tie him to a table next to the walk-in refrigerator. After tying up Lissy, Hellmac left by the rear door and took the money to the apartment they were sharing and later turned the money over to Lissy. Lissy, meanwhile, was discovered the next morning by Tom Larson when Larson opened the restaurant for business, and Lissy subsequently reported to the investigating police officers that he had been held up at gunpoint by "two black men."

Davis and Poppe were intrigued by what they had just discovered about Lissy's past life. If there had been any doubt in their minds that Lissy was responsible for Kathy's death, by now it had been completely erased. Lissy was clearly a scoundrel of the worst sort, and likely had been for most of his life. From the way things now looked, Davis and Poppe felt more confident than ever that they were on the right track. But as close as they were to the truth, they would soon discover that they had only touched the tip of the iceberg.

Ten

Larry Simpson, twenty-two, first met Michael David Lissy when he walked into the Kentucky Fried Chicken store at 1841 North Lombard Street in 1977 and applied for a job. Lissy, apparently sensing that he could use Simpson to his benefit, hired him on the spot and shortly thereafter brought him in on his "short ringing" chicken scheme.

Although Simpson never actually observed Lissy taking the money out of the till and placing it in his pocket, he said that he knew Lissy was skimming.

"He'd take it out at night, after, you know, the till was closed out and he was doing the books," Simpson said. "He'd figure how much he could take, and then take it."

"He'd give me and Joe money every night after work to, ah, you know, go have dinner or something and he'd buy pot for us and buy beer for us and pay the rent on our apartment," Simpson said. "And we knew that he couldn't do that on an assistant manager's salary."

The money, according to Simpson, amounted

to about $250 a week between the two of them. But Simpson was certain that Lissy was taking a lot more than that and was "stashing" it somewhere for later use, to use in carrying out the many schemes he'd talked about.

"This went on for about six months," Simpson said. "Then he got involved with this girl and he got married, then he decided it wasn't working out so he wanted one of us to put her out of her misery, so to speak. He wanted one of us to kill her."

Lissy began discussing the plan to kill Frankie one night at the Missouri Street house that he began sharing with Hellmac. It was an unusual arrangement in that Simpson, at one point, had moved in for a period while Frankie was living there with them, too. A number of people, especially the neighbors, thought it improper to have three men living with one woman under the same roof, even if she was married to one of them.

"He was singing the blues one night about his wife and he wanted one of us to waste her," Simpson said. "Naturally, you know, we kinda didn't want to and then after I quit, he wanted one of the other guys to waste me 'cause he thought I knew too much about him."

Simpson explained that Lissy wanted Hellmac or Donald Moore to kill him because of Simpson's knowledge that Lissy was "really taking the money heavy out of" the Killingsworth Street store. He said that he had taken the death plans seriously. However, after Lissy's embezzling schemes were discovered and he was fired, he no longer worried too much about being killed.

"From what I understand, the way he lost his job was that they found thirty some thousand dollars in a box down in the basement," Simpson said. "I believe his excuse at the time was that he hadn't, ah, been able to make a deposit because he hadn't got the books done 'til late at night and he didn't wanta, you know, make a deposit at night in that neighborhood."

When Simpson was asked about Virginia Meyer, he said that he had met her and described her as "real gangly, a skinny redhead who had a thing for black guys and stuff like that." She had been living in Northeast Portland, in a rental house that Lissy's parents owned, when Lissy met her. At one point Virginia and her family moved out of Lissy's parents' house and into the Columbia Villa on North Woolsey Street, a public housing project in a high-crime area of the city.

"Lissy and Virginia would have quiet discussions off in the back rooms, and I really never did figure it out. I remember one time he paid her and her friend, Lori, a hundred dollars to steal this stereo for us. I think they may have used Joe's car without his knowledge. I mean, well, he knew they were using the car but he didn't know what for. Lissy just asked if he could borrow the car and when Joe said, 'Sure,' then he turned the keys over to the girls and they took off. When they came back they had a really expensive Sansui with Dolby receiver, a really nice cassette deck, and a real nice turntable. A couple of weeks later it disappeared out of the apartment again, so I assume they may have stolen it back. I'm not sure."

The investigators had asked: Did Simpson know of anyone who might have been able to help Lissy accomplish the burglary of his apartment? Was Lissy capable of engineering such a scheme?

"Ah, man, is that what this is all about?" Simpson asked. "If Lissy's involved, he set it up himself, that's all I can tell ya. That's probably what the other guys told you, too. If he says he got burglarized, he did it himself, for the insurance money. I was locked up in Rocky Butte Jail at the time and I didn't even escape until May twenty-ninth, so, ah, I wouldn't know how it was accomplished. I would just know, from knowing Michael Lissy, knowing all the devious things we went through while, you know, being in contact with him. If he says he was burglarized, and he's trying to make an insurance claim, then he pulled it off himself 'cause he needed money for another one of his brilliant schemes."

What were some of Lissy's other "brilliant" schemes? The investigators wanted to know.

"Well, a lot of 'em never, you know, came off," Simpson said. "But he wanted to try running dope from Jamaica into Florida once. We got up quite a bit of money for that one and then the money just disappeared and he showed up with a brand-new Monte Carlo. He sold amphetamines out of the Lombard Street Kentucky Fried Chicken restaurant. I ate several, but I don't know who all he sold them to. Then he wanted, like I said, one of us to murder Frankie. After their divorce he either shacked up or married this other girl and wanted us to murder her mother, push her down the stairs or something, for her insurance money and the things Elise would have inherited if her mother died."

The murder plot involving Elise's mother, Sondra, germinated after Simpson had already quit working for Lissy. Lissy, Hellmac and Moore approached Simpson one day to help move some of Elise's things that were stored at her mother's house to the Killingsworth Street apartment. While moving a doll case out of the basement, Lissy called the others over and told them what he wanted them to do.

"He was telling us, you know, if one of us would be so gracious as to accidentally bump the old lady and make her fall down the stairs and die or something," Simpson said. "He said he'd make it worth our while because it would make it very much worth the girl's while if her mother were to, you know, suddenly have a demise. Elise would come into a bunch of money, and Michael being her husband would get, you know, access to it and he would make it worth our while."

Elise was not involved in the plan to kill her mother, according to Simpson. It had been

Lissy's intention to keep her in the dark about it entirely.

"Lissy said he could play the stricken man and such, and comfort Elise. Seemed like another one of his ideas, you know, if he could find somebody that was stupid enough to do it, for him to reap the profits."

Detectives Lloyd Davis and David Poppe now reasoned that Lissy probably had not killed Kathy himself. It was still possible that he had, of course, but from what they were learning about him he always seemed to find someone else to do his dirty work for him, someone he could point the finger at to take the fall for him. The two detectives wondered whom he had found that was stupid enough to murder Kathy for him.

Eleven

Francis "Frankie" Mae Schuster married Michael David Lissy on April 30, 1978, in the city of Portland. However, as would become the custom, Lissy's marriage to her did not last long, nor had he intended it to. She left him less than three months later, on July 22, when she learned of his infidelity despite the fact that she was pregnant with his child, due to be born in the third week of October. Frankie had discovered that Lissy was committing adultery and having various affairs with women and young girls, including Virginia and Elise. Frankie filed for divorce, sued Lissy for paternity in the matter of the child, which he denied was his, and the divorce was finally granted on July 5, 1979, freeing Lissy to marry Elise Dunn shortly thereafter. Frankie, a Roman Catholic, also went through the process of having the marriage annulled by the Church.

It was by now obvious to Detectives Lloyd Davis and David Poppe that Lissy had established a pattern of marrying a new wife just as soon as possible after tying up the loose ends and receiving a divorce decree from the previous spouse. It had been no different when Kathy came along, but the detectives continued to wonder how he had convinced Kathy to make him beneficiary of her life-insurance policy before his divorce with Elise had become final. Lissy was indeed an amazing man. A scoundrel, for sure, but no less amazing.

According to investigative reports, Lissy had not been able to provide any record of his divorce from his first wife in Seattle, Washington, at the time he and Frankie Schuster decided to get married. According to Frankie's statements, Lissy had told her several versions, each different, of what had happened to his first wife. On one occasion he told her that his first wife was dead, and another time told Frankie that she was alive. He said that he had a daughter named Angela and claimed that she was dead, too, and at one point showed Frankie a letter on the letterhead of Nicholas Birnbaum, M.D.*, which suggested that his first wife was dead. Naturally, Frankie didn't know what to believe. Unfortunately, she was unable to locate the letter for the investigators.

However, when Frankie petitioned the Church for an annulment of her marriage to Lissy, she hired a private investigator to look into his marital status. Even without the "lost" letter on Dr. Birnbaum's stationery, the investigator was able to determine that it was in all likelihood a forgery, but got no further than that. Frankie persisted, however, and learned from Lissy's parents, whom she described as very wealthy and living in a very expensive house near the town of Depoe Bay along the Oregon coast, that the first wife was still alive and residing somewhere in Seattle. She found out that there had been no child from that marriage, and that Lissy had been going by his real name, Michael David Reid, at the time of the marriage to the Washington woman.

Frankie confirmed much of what Larry Simpson, Joe Hellmac and the others had said about Lissy's activities, and she naturally had a very poor opinion of her former husband. Shortly after the "robbery" of the Kentucky Fried Chicken restaurant, Lissy began flashing a large wad of money. When she asked him about it, Lissy told her that he had won $1,200 in a horse race. She said that ever since she left Lissy, she had feared retribution from him and feared for her personal safety. After winning the paternity suit against Lissy and obtaining a judgment for child-support payments, Frankie said that she entered into an agreement with Lissy to waive the support payments so that she could stop his visitation rights with their child. She no longer wanted him to see or have any contact with the child, and stated that she felt that Lissy was in dire need of a mental-health professional. Frankie described Lissy as a sociopathic liar, and felt that he didn't realize some of the things he did.

"He cannot tell the truth even to protect himself," she said. Although she believed that Lissy was "off the deep end," he was nonetheless a very convincing smooth talker and regularly told lies which he himself believed were true. He also always "picked" on younger people because he knew they were more "gullible" and easily persuaded by his slickness.

Among the lies that Lissy told was the claim that he owned an island in the Caribbean and had several businesses there, which he operated with his grandfather. Right before they were married he claimed that he had a multimillion-dollar inheritance coming to him from a relative that had died. As she had come to expect, this had turned out to be untrue, as had most of Lissy's claims; the relative who died had no money. He had also told her that he had a lot of money coming in from extensive rental properties he owned in Portland and from various other businesses, but again it was just another lie. The rental properties belonged to Lissy's mother and stepfather, who also owned motels and other real estate on the Oregon coast. In an attempt to ward off being found out, he had always handled all of the money and always told Frankie that he was reinvesting it. As a result she never saw or handled any of his money.

In the meantime, Lissy began setting the stage for Elise. While Lissy and Frankie were in the process of obtaining their divorce, Lissy apparently took Elise to a marina on the Columbia River near Jantzen Beach in North Portland and showed her three boats which he said Frankie had taken from him in the divorce. He apparently also told Elise that Frankie had gotten an airplane that he said he owned, which was supposedly located in The Dalles, Oregon. He also told her that he was paying $1,800 a month in alimony and child support to Frankie. Of course, all of this was eventually proven to be untrue.

After Frankie and Lissy split up, Lissy claimed Frankie and their child as dependents on his federal income-tax return for 1978, even though he had not provided any of their upkeep or support. When Frankie found out about it she reported him to the Internal Revenue Service, which sparked an investigation and an audit in which Lissy was denied the filing status that he had claimed. As a result, he owed additional federal and state income taxes for the 1978 tax year.

Frankie reiterated the fact that Lissy had insured her life for $50,000, with a double-indemnity clause shortly before their separation. She had subsequently heard from Joe Hellmac and Tom Larson that Lissy was planning to "make sure she had an accident" and died. Even though she didn't know whether it was the truth or just a sick joke, the information had frightened her tremendously and she had made sure that the insurance was canceled when she left Lissy.

* * *

Additional background information, specifically records pertaining to Lissy's employment history, indicated that Lissy had worked for a number of companies throughout the Pacific Northwest. Lissy had claimed to have worked for Sea Breeze Construction Company in Depoe Bay, Oregon; Oregon Greenhouse Company in Dufur, Oregon; and Melrose Bakery in Seattle, Washington. However, the detectives were unable to locate any of those businesses. Similarly, Lissy had listed several companies, many of which were fast-food restaurants and convenience stores, that had gone out of business years earlier, making it difficult to verify whether he had actually worked for the companies or not. Similarly, he reported that he had worked for Bell Telephone Company in Seattle, but the company told the detectives that they had no record that he had ever worked for them. The list went on and on.

Only one company, Moore-Oregon International, turned up records that verified Lissy's employment. Lissy had worked for that company from September 1978 to November 1978, and during that short time span the quality of his work had been reported as good. He had not been laid off, nor had he been disciplined or fired. He apparently had been involved in an industrial accident there, which involved a back sprain, but he had not incurred any lost time.

Public agency reports disclosed that, in addition to the "armed robbery" of the Kentucky

Fried Chicken restaurant and the "burglaries" at Lissy's residences, Lissy had also experienced the following problems: On May 21, 1976, Lissy had been the victim of an armed robbery on a public parking lot in downtown Portland. He claimed that he had lost his cash, wallet, and credit cards. Around midnight on November 3, 1976, Lissy had been stopped and questioned by police at Southwest Twelfth Avenue and Taylor Street, also in downtown Portland, while in the company of two felons known to the Portland Police Bureau as having been involved in various crimes and thefts. One of the investigating officers described the felons as a white man who was known to be a transvestite and burglar, and a woman who had previous convictions as a thief.

On May 11, 1977, Lissy experienced another armed robbery, also of his person, at 425 Northeast Clackamas Street in Portland, in which he claimed to have had his cash, wallet, and credit cards stolen. On November 1, 1978, Lissy was arrested for driving while his license was suspended. On February 15, 1979, Lissy was arrested on a bench warrant for failure to appear in court on an automobile hazard violation. On February 7, 1980, Elise Lissy was the victim of a hit-and-run accident which occurred at 11195 Southwest Capitol Highway in Portland. Although Lissy reeked of fraud, neither he nor his wife, Elise, had any record of prior criminal convictions.

Although Lissy was listed as the owner of the Valley Windsurfing and Scuba Shops at the time of Kathy's murder, Davis and Poppe had uncovered information which showed that Lissy had made claims in April 1981 to being only a "minority partner" in the business where he was then "self-employed" as a scuba instructor. The owner at that time, they learned, was listed as Ray Thomas*. Although Lissy had wholly taken over the business sometime after 1981, the detectives thought it might be interesting to probe Lissy's earlier relationship with the business.

Ray Thomas, twenty-five, a blond, corpulent man, told the detectives that Lissy had loaned him $2,000 in June 1980, which Thomas used to help keep the business afloat financially. He said that he had repaid the debt by May 1981. According to Thomas, Lissy taught swimming lessons, served as a dive coordinator, and as an assistant instructor at the center, then known only as the Valley Scuba Center, but did so wholly as a volunteer and received no compensation for his work. Lissy paid for a number of lessons for himself and Elise, and also purchased approximately $10,000 worth of scuba-diving equipment in 1980 for which he paid cash. Thomas said that Lissy always paid for his purchases with cash and always carried "a lot of cash in his pocket." Lissy apparently always led Thomas to believe that he had a great deal of money that he obtained from his family, and had stated on more than one occasion that he had all the money he needed. It appeared that Thomas had been somewhat dependent upon Lissy for his volunteer labor and access to cash up to the time that Lissy purchased the business from him.

Dr. Nicholas Birnbaum was eventually located in Seattle through the Professional Licensing Division of the State of Washington. At first Dr. Birnbaum was extremely cautious about discussing any matter involving Michael David Lissy, known to Birnbaum as Michael David Reid. However, Birnbaum relaxed somewhat when he learned that the detectives were seeking information that only pertained to them locating Lissy's first wife.

Birnbaum said that he last saw Lissy in 1972. At that time Lissy was going by his real name of Reid. He didn't know Lissy's wife's name, but he had met her on one or two occasions. He recalled being at Lissy's home in North Seattle on one occasion, but didn't remember the address. Birnbaum knew nothing of the allegedly forged letter on Birnbaum's letterhead that Lissy had shown Frankie. He certainly hadn't written it, but it was possible that Lissy had obtained several sheets of his letterhead from his office. Birnbaum added that he thought the detectives were "on the right track" and felt that they should "pursue" the investigation rigorously. He provided them with the name of a person he felt might know the location of the former "Mrs. Reid."

As a result of the new contact, the investigators learned that Lissy had been married to a woman named Martha, whose maiden name was apparently Carlson. Martha "Reid" was traced to a former employer in downtown Seattle, and an official at the company recalled that the "Reids" had lived in a ranch-style house in the Edmonds, Washington area, near Seattle. The company official recalled that Reid/Lissy had become involved with another woman in 1972, and she thought that the affair might have led to the Reids' divorce.

Additional investigation indicated that Martha was Lissy's first wife. It appeared that they were married in Washington in the late 1960s, and divorced in King County, Washington, sometime in 1972, perhaps later. However, the King County Recorder's Office at the King County Courthouse, Marriage License Department, in Seattle, had no records that pertained to Martha Reid and/or Michael Reid. Despite the fact that Lissy had told several people stories about his first wife, including that she was deceased and that they'd had a daughter who was also deceased, the detectives were unable to locate her or verify whether she was alive or dead. It was baffling, and it seemed like the former Martha Reid had vanished from the face of the earth. Davis and Poppe resigned themselves to the possibility that she was another mysterious facet of Lissy's life that might not ever be fully disclosed or understood.

Twelve

As they continued to peer into Michael David Lissy's past, Detectives Lloyd Davis and David Poppe found additional documentation relating to the purported break-in and burglary of Lissy's Northeast Killingsworth apartment on the weekend of April 3–5, 1981. Among the items reported as stolen were two color televisions, a Radio Shack TRS-80 computer, a Panasonic videotape camera, recorder/player and related video equipment, several stereo components, a microwave oven, a food processor, a Vivitar photographic enlarger, an outboard motor, inflatable rafts, bicycles, and credit cards. All-in-all, the claim was for more than $11,000 worth of various items. They also found a recorded statement taken by a property adjuster with Farmers Insurance Company.

In the recorded statement, Lissy had told the adjuster that all of the items that had been stolen were free and clear. None of the items were financed or being held as collateral, and Lissy pointed out that he paid cash for nearly everything he bought. It was clear from the adjuster's tone that he found this particularly difficult to believe, especially when he inquired about Lissy's income.

"Do you remember what your income was for 1980? Both yours and your wife's?" the adjuster had asked.

"Uh, it was about four or five thousand dollars."

"The income. Your total income."

"Yeah."

"Four or five thousand dollars is all you made in 1980?"

"Correct."

"How did you buy all of these things? Have you had them a while?"

"Most of them are new," Lissy had said. "We bought them with savings."

"I see. You've had some savings that you've dug into."

In response to the adjuster's questions, Lissy had explained that he and Elise had lived at the apartment for a couple of years, and during that time they had witnessed a burglary and theft at the complex. That, he had said, was what had prompted them to purchase a renter's insurance policy. As to their whereabouts at the time of the burglary, Lissy explained that he, Elise, and a friend, Paul McNeil, had gone to Bridgeport, Washington, for the weekend to go scuba-diving in the Hood Canal. They stayed at a motel there that was popular with scuba divers. Davis and Poppe noted that Lissy's story regarding his whereabouts at the time his apartment was burglarized had checked out. His friend, Paul McNeil, 39, had corroborated the trip to Bridgeport for the insurance investigators.

The manager of the apartment complex had characterized Lissy and his wife as excellent renters. They had always been very quiet, and they had always paid their rent on time. But by this time Davis and Poppe knew that the characterizations of Lissy as an upstanding, respectable citizen were nothing more than a phony facade that he had deliberately created. Many of the people interviewed by the insurance investigator believed, of course, that Lissy was a good guy. But it was still a facade, and the detectives were more determined than ever to prove it.

Davis and Poppe soon discovered a letter dated November 4, 1981, from a law firm representing Farmers Insurance Company which pointedly raised suspicions about Lissy's claim but which ultimately, albeit reluctantly, supported it.

Lissy, the detectives discovered, was subsequently paid more than $11,000 for the loss by Farmers Insurance Company. The claim was listed as closed.

On Friday, July 20, 1984, Eugene police detective Michael Marsh went to the Valley River Inn with photographs of Michael and Kathy Lissy that had been obtained as part of the ongoing investigation. He showed them to several hotel employees, to see if anybody recalled seeing Lissy or the victim on July 5–6. Many reported having seen the victim, but he struck out on Lissy with each employee until he reached Bonita Jean Golliher, the night maintenance supervisor. When Marsh showed Golliher the photos of Kathy and Lissy, she indicated that she had previously been shown a photograph of the victim. However, she positively identified Lissy as a person whom she had seen in the hotel's lobby sometime between midnight, July 5, and 12:30 A.M. July 6. The last time she saw him he was walking from the staircase area toward the main doors to exit the hotel lobby. She told Marsh that he was wearing faded blue jeans, a short-sleeved dark blue or perhaps black shirt, and noted that he was a very large man.

Davis and Poppe were not surprised by the information when Detective Marsh relayed it to them, but they were delighted at the new development. Since Lissy's photo had not yet appeared in the news media, it was a reasonable assumption that Golliher's memory would not have been unduly triggered unless she had actually seen him in person, thus making her identification of his photo more than likely accurate. The development had taken them one step closer to being able to nail Lissy for his wife's murder. Noting that Eugene was only one hundred or so miles from Lake Oswego, Davis and

Poppe reasoned that Lissy could have made the trip to Eugene in less than two hours while driving the legal speed limit. He had said that he was at home, passed out from drinking, by 9:30 or 10 P.M., the detectives recalled. If he had lied to them about passing out, he could have easily arrived in Eugene by midnight.

On July 23, 1984, Davis contacted Melvin Reese in Texas after several failed attempts to reach him. Reese, he learned, was an old boyfriend of Kathy's, and he had given Kathy a gold necklace that she nearly always wore. Davis recalled that the necklace, which was not on her body when it was found by Martha Chamberlin in the hotel room, had been described in earlier interviews by Lissy. Reese said the necklace consisted of a gold pendant in a "V" shape, with one bar on one side and two bars on the other. There was also a small diamond where the "V" came to a point.

Whoever had the necklace, reasoned Davis, likely killed Kathy. He listed the necklace, along with her checkbook, wallet, and credit cards, among other items such as the clothing Lissy was believed wearing the night of the murder, as items to be seized if found during the execution of a search warrant he was preparing.

From that point on, Davis and Poppe focused on Lissy as their prime suspect. They didn't really know what lay ahead, but they were going to find out. They began to dig around the streets of Portland, trying to find other people who knew something, anything, about the case. They found several.

Thirteen

Early on Tuesday morning, July 24, 1984, Detectives Lloyd Davis and David Poppe again drove to Portland, search warrants in hand. Their plan was to search the condominium that Michael David Lissy had shared with Kathy; they were also going to search his business at 10803 S.W. Barbur Boulevard, in which he maintained his office, and an apartment at 10800 S.W. Barbur Boulevard, directly across the street from the scuba-diving shop. The apartment, unit number sixteen, had formerly been rented by Elise Dunn. However, she had turned the apartment over to Lissy, and the manager earlier told the detectives that Lissy had paid for his July rent at the first of the month. But before they commenced with the searches, they first wanted to talk to Elise. When they showed up at the downtown Portland offices where Elise had worked for the past four and a half years as an accountant, she met them and took them into a room where they could talk privately.

Elise, then twenty-seven, told the detectives that she had learned accounting by doing the books at the Valley Windsurfing and Scuba Shops, which had eventually enabled her to obtain her present job. She explained that she had known Lissy since 1978, and married him the summer of 1979. They were divorced in December, 1983, she said, and Lissy married Kathryn Martini on January 28, 1984. Elise explained that she learned of Kathy's murder some two weeks earlier, on Saturday, July 7, when she called Lissy about a prearranged meeting between them and he told her about it.

"Michael and I were supposed to meet that day to go over the books for Valley Scuba, but we hadn't set a time," Elise said. "I called him at home around eleven or eleven-thirty that morning to find out when we were going to get together to go over the books, and that is when he informed me that Kathy had been killed. He said that she had been strangled."

She explained that she had done the books for Lissy's business from November 1981 to July 1984. Lissy, she said, had asked her to under-record sales for June and July of 1984, and then asked her to decrease the sales for July even further—by some $2,000. He had not told her why he wanted the books tampered with, but the detectives figured and Elise confirmed that he had wanted to remove cash from the business, like he had done on so many occasions at the Kentucky Fried Chicken restaurants he had managed.

"Oftentimes sales weren't recorded and he

would pocket the cash from the sales," she said,
indicating that he didn't have to tell her *why* he
wanted the books juggled. If there was a particularly large sale, Lissy had often asked her to
underreport each large sale by amounts that
ranged from $500 to $1,000. "And oftentimes
he would take money from the till before I had
a chance to do the accounting. There was no
way to balance the cash for the books."

She told the detectives that Lissy had an unusually insatiable sexual appetite and that he
frequently hired prostitutes to service him sexually, as many as two or three times a day. On
some occasions, Elise was personally present
when Lissy hired prostitutes to have sex with
him.

"I saw him give quite a bit of it (the money)
to prostitutes," she said.

After a moment or two of silence, as if she
were deep in thought, Elise asked the detectives:
"What room was Kathy killed in at the Valley
River Inn?" Davis and Poppe looked at each
other briefly before responding.

"Room 305," Davis said. "Why?"

Elise appeared somewhat shaken by Davis's response, but not particularly surprised. Slowly,
she took out a piece of paper she had been carrying in her purse. It was red in color with black
lettering on the front, approximately eight and
a half inches wide by five and a half inches long,
about half the size of a normal eight-and-a-half
by eleven-inches sheet of paper. It was a sale

flyer for Valley Windsurfing and Scuba Shops, advertising a "Lucky Day Sale" for July 13, 1984, noon to midnight, in which everything in the stores were twenty-five percent off. It was the type of flyer that would be given to customers when they came in or as they left one of the shops. However, when Davis turned it over, the detectives saw "305" hand-printed on the back side.

"I thought it connected Michael Lissy with the murder," Elise said.

"Where did you get this?" Poppe asked.

"The Saturday that I found out Kathy had been killed," she said, "Michael asked me to go over to the condominium, and he took me into the bedroom and he gave me this piece of paper and said he wanted me to destroy it." She explained that it was tucked inside an envelope when Lissy handed it to her, and she had just put it in her pocket at the time without looking to see what the envelope contained.

"Couple of hours later he told me it was a phone number of Kathy's drug connection," Elise continued. "He didn't want it to be brought out. It would be an embarrassment for the family if they knew she used drugs. I put it in the pocket of my jeans. Couple of hours later in the rest room I took it out and looked at it, and it was just three numbers. I thought, 'Why would he write an extension down without writing the whole phone number down?' So I asked him about it. He said it was a room number. I asked if it was Kathy's room number and he said, 'No, it is a room number of a hotel here in Portland, the Hamilton, where you can go to buy drugs or sex or whatever you want.' I put it back in my pocket. And a couple of weeks later I put on those jeans. I forgot about it. And it bothered me that it was just a little short number."

Elise explained that when Lissy gave her the piece of paper on Saturday, July 7, he knew that the police were coming to see him at the condominium to talk to him.

"He told me they would be coming up that afternoon to talk to him," she said. Lissy wanted her to take the note because he feared that the police were going to arrive at any time and would search the condominium. At that time he had no way of knowing that the search was still more than two weeks away. However, he was in for quite a surprise that very afternoon.

Elise told the detectives that she knew Lissy's business was heavily in debt, that he owed upward of $100,000 to manufacturers. He was also behind in his payments to the former owner, who was threatening to take over the business when she quit for good in the early part of July, shortly after learning of Kathy's murder.

Elise explained that, at Lissy's insistence, she and Lissy had participated in two "fake" burglaries so that Lissy would be able to recover large sums of money from his insurance company. One of those engineered burglaries occurred at their apartment on North Killingsworth Street in April 1981, she said, and the other occurred in March 1984 at the scuba business on Barbur Boulevard. In the March 1984 burglary, more than $58,000 worth of scuba gear was reported missing by Lissy.

At one point Elise told the detectives about some mysterious phone calls she had received from a woman. They were basically of a threatening nature and demanded that Elise "play ball and keep her mouth shut," or face exposure of some of her previous activities that she wasn't particularly proud of. She suspected that Lissy was behind those calls, apparently afraid to make them himself. It suddenly became clear to Davis and Poppe that Elise had been the mystery woman called by Molly Griggs, for which Molly had been paid by Lissy.

Davis and Poppe now saw those phone calls for what they were, a form of blackmail and intimidation. Elise held a responsible job as an accountant for a large company and, of course, Lissy knew that exposing unflattering moments from Elise's past would embarrass her and perhaps even cause her serious problems at work. By the time that Lissy paid Molly to make the calls to Elise, he knew that the police would be suspecting him for Kathy's murder. And her knowledge of his past schemes would only serve to damage any kind of defense he was planning to make. So he had to keep her quiet, if possible. Naturally, Elise would be inclined to play along for a while, not wanting her involvement with the previous episodes of insurance fraud exposed. Insurance fraud wouldn't look good for someone in her position. She had no desire to go to jail for crimes that Lissy had engineered.

Elise stressed the importance of keeping her job. She was paying off a credit-union loan that she had obtained for Lissy, a large loan which he was supposed to have made payments on but hadn't. Unfortunately for Elise, he hadn't signed the loan agreement papers with her, which prevented the credit union from going after him for the debt. It was yet another example in which Lissy had used someone to get what he wanted for himself without regard for what would happen to the other person. Because the payments were taken right out of her check on payday and consisted of more than half of her monthly salary, Elise said she had been forced to take a second job working in a Portland massage parlor. Because of her need to make up the money lost to Lissy so that she could pay her own bills, she also had agreed to perform sexual services on Lissy for money after their divorce. The practice continued while Lissy was married to Kathy, and even after Kathy's death. Elise, however, had recently ceased to engage in sex with Lissy because she believed that he was somehow involved in Kathy's death. She told Davis and Poppe that she feared for her own life.

When asked why she thought Lissy was involved in Kathy's murder, Elise said that Lissy had told her, prior to their divorce, that he was divorcing her to marry Kathryn Ann Martini. It was his plan, she said, to marry Kathy for her money and to be able to use Kathy's banking connections to obtain a loan for his business. He had stressed to Elise that after he had obtained what he wanted from Kathy, he would end his liaison with her and come back to Elise. Lissy's plans never worked out for him, however, in that he never got the loans he wanted from any of Kathy's connections. And when she learned that Kathy had been strangled and Lissy had given her the piece of paper with the number "305" written on it, she just somehow knew that he had to be involved in the murder.

Davis and Poppe thanked her for her time and cooperation, and informed her that they would likely have more questions for her later.

After leaving Elise Dunn's place of employment, the two detectives checked with the Portland Police Bureau on the status of the burglary at Lissy's business. As a result of their inquiry they learned that Portland detectives had found some of the stolen scuba gear on May 22, stashed away inside a self-storage unit located at 5803 Southeast 122nd Avenue in Portland. The case was still under investigation, but Portland detectives hadn't been able to positively link Lissy to the burglary. After Elise's statements to Davis and Poppe, however, that could all change very quickly.

In part because of Elise's statements about the April 1981 burglary, Paul McNeil was now implicated. As a result McNeil, now wanting to cooperate, would later tell authorities that he had been employed by Lissy at a Plaid Pantry convenience store that Lissy and Elise had managed. He said that he had helped Lissy steal money and goods from the store and that Lissy had paid him $1,000 for helping transfer the money and goods. Facing the facts, McNeil now told the truth and admitted that he had helped "clean out" Lissy and Elise's apartment and had transferred furniture and household appliances to a rental storage unit in 1981, and for these services Lissy had paid him with a nineteen-inch color television. It was now clear that McNeil had not been truthful in his statements to the insurance investigator. He had not only helped Lissy remove and hide the stolen items, he had lied to help Lissy establish an alibi and collect the insurance money.

Try as they might during the course of their intensive investigation, Davis and Poppe were unable to confirm much of anything that Lissy had told them and others about his life and background. Lissy clearly wasn't everything that he had made himself out to be. In fact, he didn't even come close. He had two scuba shops in Portland, both of which were doing extremely badly. He was over $100,000 in debt and was considering bankruptcy. They had determined that he held no contracts with any agency or branch of the federal government, and the National Geographic Society had never heard of him, not even for a membership or a subscription order. Instead, Davis and Poppe were seeing that Lissy was a "particularly degenerate" individual who placed money at the top of his priorities. The detectives agreed that the reason for Kathy's murder was pure and simple greed: Lissy hoped to collect on her life-insurance policies, which they knew she had but which Lissy had denied any knowledge of; insurance policies which, with the multiplier clause on her salary, would net the beneficiary nearly $200,000, if Kathy happened to die while traveling on business.

At 4:25 that afternoon, July 24, Detectives Davis, Poppe, J.T. Parr, Wayne Irvin, and two other officers from the Eugene Police Department converged on Lissy's condominium at 128 Oswego Summit in Lake Oswego, armed with search warrants. They hoped to find "an instrument capable of leaving a 'Y'-shaped impression about 1" long" on the victim's head; a gold necklace with a gold, "V"-shaped pendant; written documentation of any agreement or any payment for the commission of Kathy's murder; receipts for the purchase of gasoline in or between the cities of Lake Oswego and Eugene on July 5 and July 6, 1984, by Lissy or anyone closely associated with him; evidence of any insurance policies on Kathy's life naming Lissy as the beneficiary; Kathy's credit cards; Kathy's Oregon driver's license; a dark blue or black woman's wallet; Kathy's address book; a short-sleeved blue or black men's shirt; and a pair of men's faded blue jeans.

"We need to talk to you," Davis told Lissy when Lissy answered the front door. Lissy beckoned them inside to the living-room area, where Davis informed him that they were there to serve and execute a search warrant. Lissy, shaken and obviously upset, turned pale and sat down on the sofa.

Davis then advised Lissy of his Miranda rights, and when asked if he understood those rights Lissy indicated that he did. Davis then read the search warrant to Lissy, and Poppe informed him that they had talked to various witnesses who had provided them with information that led them to suspect Lissy of being involved in the murder of his wife.

"We talked with your ex-wife Elise," Poppe said. "And we talked with Molly Griggs. We have tapes of your conversations with Molly." Lissy remained seated on the couch, and continued to look at Poppe but did not say much.

At one point Poppe showed Lissy a piece of their evidence, the envelope that contained the folded advertisement with the number "305" handwritten on the back side that they had received from Elise earlier that day.

"Do you recognize this item?" Poppe asked. Lissy did not answer verbally, but nodded his head up and down.

"You were seen at the Valley River Inn on the Thursday night that your wife was killed," Poppe said. Again, Lissy did not speak, but denied Poppe's statement by shaking his head from side to side.

"Are you willing to talk to us about this?" Davis asked.

"No," Lissy said, effectively invoking his rights against self-incrimination. At that point the detectives and officers began the search of the premises. Poppe remained with Lissy to make certain that he did not attempt to destroy any evidence.

Lissy, at one point, got up and made a telephone call. A short time later his attorney, Michael Sturgeon, arrived at the condominium.

"Am I under arrest?" Lissy asked.

"No, you are not," Poppe replied. Poppe stayed with him for a while longer, then traded off with another detective and assisted in the search.

While searching behind a bureau in the master bedroom, Poppe found a receipt that was dated July 6, 1984, the same day that Kathy's body was discovered at the Valley River Inn. The receipt was from the Oregon First Bank made out in the amount of $116. It interested Poppe because it had handwritten figures on the back side that totaled $9,800. Its significance, if any, was not known.

Nearby, Detective Parr was searching through a utility closet, a large walk-through area between the second bedroom and the upstairs bathroom where Kathy also apparently had done her ironing. It was while looking along a shelf inside the closet directly above the ironing board that he found a large gray envelope, which was clearly marked, "Insurance Policies." He took the envelope over to Poppe.

When they looked inside they found a five-page handwritten note on stationery from Harold's Club Casino in Reno that was entitled, "Last will of K.A. Martini," which made Lissy the sole beneficiary of her estate. In an addendum to the will, Kathryn had removed her parents' names and had added Lissy with regard to the insurance she carried. There were several other insurance papers, including a pink sheet that listed Michael Lissy as the "100 percent beneficiary" for the insurance. Poppe and Parr went out to the living room, where Davis was now conferring with Lissy's attorney and observing the movements of their suspect. Poppe handed the will to Davis.

"What's that?" Lissy asked, a surprised look on his face.

"It's your wife's will," Poppe said, stone-faced.

"Where did you find it?" Lissy asked.

"I didn't find it. Detective Parr found it inside a closet."

Poppe and Parr, now accompanied by Detective Irvin, returned to the closet where Parr had found the envelope of insurance papers. As Parr placed the envelope back in the area from where he had retrieved it, Irvin took a photograph to show where Parr had found it and to show just how accessible it had been to anyone looking for such papers. Lissy had previously told them that he had no idea what, if any, type of insurance Kathy had.

While searching the kitchen, Poppe found a small address book, approximately three by four inches with a unicorn on the front, in a drawer to the left of the stove area. Kathy's name was on the front inside page. While thumbing through it, Poppe recognized several names that he knew were friends and relatives of Kathy's. He took the address book out to the living room, just as he had done with the envelope containing the insurance documents.

"Where did you find that?" Lissy asked when Poppe came into view.

"Inside a drawer in the kitchen," Poppe responded. Lissy identified the address book as Kathy's, but told the detective that he hadn't seen it in a long time.

"Is this the same address book which you previously described as having been among Kathy's missing property?" Poppe asked.

Lissy explained that the address book that he had reported missing was dark blue, perhaps even black, and was more formal-looking than the one that Poppe had found.

"Do you mean that the book you just described is the same as Kathy's missing wallet?" Poppe asked, who recalled that the description of Kathy's missing wallet was the same or similar to the description that Lissy had just provided. But Lissy did not immediately respond.

"That was the description of the wallet that I heard," Poppe said.

"One or the other," Lissy responded, now perhaps confused. Poppe didn't press the issue any further.

The search warrant they had served on Lissy also included the right to search Lissy's blue Chevy van, Oregon license plate number CTL 507, which Lissy owned and used in his business. They found it parked in the residential-parking area nearby. Sturgeon and Lissy stood by and watched as Davis conducted the search.

At one point Davis called out to Poppe, who was standing just outside the sliding side door. He pointed out to Poppe a side locker, located to the left and slightly behind the driver's seat. Davis opened it. Inside the locker they found a bag, inside of which was something wrapped up in a towel. When they removed the bag and its contents, they discovered a .357 magnum revolver. The gun, a Colt Python with a two-and-a-half-inch barrel, was fully loaded with six rounds of ammunition. Poppe unloaded the gun, placed the bullets in a bag, and marked it appropriately. Poppe then beckoned Lissy over to the van.

"Is this your revolver?" he asked as he showed the gun to Lissy.

"Yes, it is," Lissy said.

"Where did you obtain it?"

Lissy explained that he had traded it with "some guy" for a scuba tank at one of his stores, but he didn't know the person's name. He told Poppe that a receipt probably existed at one of the stores, but he wasn't certain about that.

"When did you make the trade?" Poppe asked.

"About three to four months ago," Lissy said.

"Do you have a concealed weapons permit?"

"No."

Poppe subsequently called in the gun's serial number to the Portland Police Bureau. After running a check through their computer system, they informed Poppe that the gun had been stolen in a theft from a Washington County home on or about June 18, 1984, well short of the "three or four months ago" like Lissy had said.

The search warrant also gave the detectives the authority to search the apartment on Barbur Boulevard, across the street from one of Lissy's shops. The apartment, they learned from witnesses, had been occupied by Lissy and Elise Dunn, where they carried out some of their sexual liaisons. But Elise had moved out, leaving Lissy with possession of the apartment. By the time they finished their search of the apartment, they had found additional scuba gear that hadn't been recovered from the self-storage unit by Portland police in May, but which they nonetheless believed was part of the $58,000 burglary in March. That equipment was turned over to Portland Police Bureau Detective Paul Fink. They also found twenty-three photographs depicting nude women and men which they deemed pornographic.

Before they finished for the day, the detectives also seized a financial statement from Lissy's Barbur Boulevard shop listing himself and Kathryn, and the Bank of Milwaukie, Oregon.

"This is all like a bad dream," Lissy said.

Fourteen

Detectives Lloyd Davis and David Poppe soon learned that the Bank of Milwaukie, which was listed on the financial statement seized at Michael Lissy's office at the Barbur Boulevard scuba shop, was an independent bank that had been bought by the U.S. National Bank of Oregon a month earlier, in June 1984. Seeking additional information about Lissy's finances, the detectives contacted Millard Sinclair, vice president and district manager of the U.S. National Bank of Oregon.

Sinclair, responding to their queries, told the detectives that Lissy and Kathy had come to the then Bank of Milwaukie in October 1983, seeking a loan for business expansion purposes. They had apparently been referred to the bank by a local accounting firm, who were also customers of the bank. Not yet married, they had applied for a $50,000 loan. Kathy's background in banking, they reasoned, had served as an advantage to Lissy because Kathy possessed a clear understanding of what criteria were needed to obtain the kind of loan for which they had applied. However, although Kathy's income was such that she could take care of herself without any money from Lissy, their assets weren't sufficient enough for the bank to grant them the loan they requested, according to Sinclair.

It soon became apparent to Davis and Poppe that Molly Griggs wasn't the only person who had information that implicated Michael David Lissy in Kathy's murder. Word on the street, they learned, was that he had solicited a number of people besides Molly to find him a hit man who would carry out his dirty work. Trouble was, how many of these street people would make reliable witnesses? Many of them were prostitutes, drug addicts, and petty criminals, some of whom were, themselves, wanted by the police on a variety of charges. Could they be made to talk? And if so, would they tell the truth? Davis and Poppe had serious doubts about that, but they had little choice and virtually nowhere else to go since these were Lissy's "friends," the people with whom he preferred to associate. They had to rely on these people if they were going to be able to build a strong enough case to prosecute Lissy for his wife's murder.

Along those lines Davis and Poppe soon learned about a young woman named Beth Cumley*, then twenty-two, a sometimes prostitute who had worked for Lissy at his scuba shops. Their relationship had started off innocuously enough, but eventually one thing had led to another and she had ended up a little more intimately involved with Lissy than she had wanted or planned.

Beth first met Lissy through a friend who had introduced them toward the end of 1982. That initial meeting occurred in downtown Portland at a place for hot-tubbing called Just for the Health of It, and the meeting turned out to be for sexual activity for which Lissy paid her $50. The sexual liaisons for pay continued in an on-and-off manner for some time, with $50 being the standard payment, until Lissy eventually asked Beth to work for him at his shops for an hourly wage. She began working for him in May 1983 for $4 per hour. When he paid her for her work, the check would often include payment for doing other things at the scuba shops, personal errands, and sometimes sexual favors. Sometimes, she said, Lissy would tell her, "If you want your check, you are going to have to do something sexual before you get it."

Then, in April 1984, Lissy asked her a question which had disturbed her immensely.

"He asked me, off the wall, if I'd ever kill anybody for ten thousand dollars," said Beth. "I told him there was no way, that life means more than money to me, that I wouldn't do anything like that. Nobody's life is worth any amount of money . . . he mentioned to me that if you want to get anywhere in life, you have to do it illegally." Beth quit working for Lissy around the middle

Kathryn Ann Martini-Lissy, 26, victim, was strangled to death in her hotel room while on a business trip.

Kathryn married Michael David Lissy, 34, after a whirlwind courtship in January, 1984.

The Valley River Inn, the four-star hotel in Eugene, Oregon
where Kathryn's body was found.

Kathryn's new sports car was found in the same
space she'd parked it on the day she checked into
The Valley River Inn.

Kathryn's pants, stripped from her body, were found on the floor next to the bed where her body was found. Investigators also found a moistened tampon to the left of the night table despite the fact that Kathryn was not into her menstrual cycle at the time of her death.

The body of Kathryn Ann Martini-Lissy as discovered by the hotel maid Martha Chamberlin.

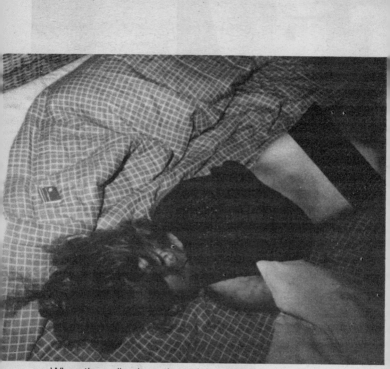

When the police investigated the scene, they found a hotel matchbook on the bed next to Kathryn's body. This small detail became significant when David Wilson told Tina LaPlante, acting undercover for the police, that he'd left a matchbook on the bed near Kathryn's body—a fact known only to police at the time.

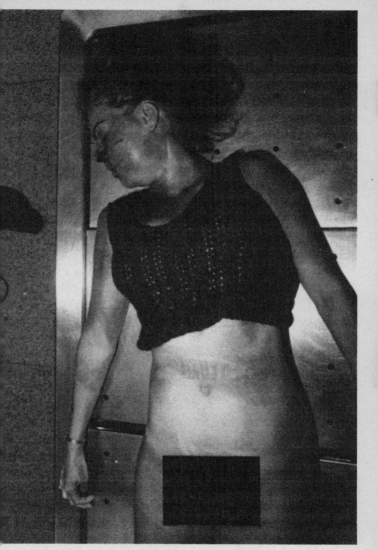

Martini's body on the autopsy table of the Lane County Medical Examiner.

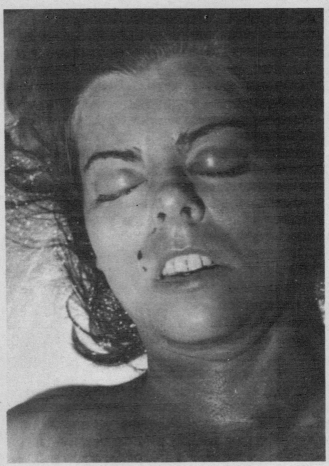
Due to the savagery of the murder, Kathryn's body and
face needed to be cleaned before an autopsy
could be performed.

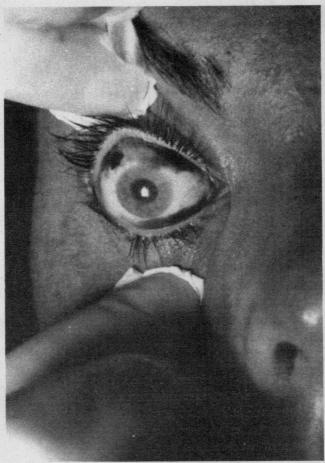

Hemorrhaging of the eyes, a condition typical of strangulation victims, was found by Dr. Edmund Wilson, Lane County Medical Examiner.

While searching the home of Michael and Kathryn Lissy, Detective J.T. Parr discovered an envelope containing several insurance policies on Kathryn's life listing Michael as the beneficiary and a will written in Kathryn's own hand leaving everything she owned to her husband.

Lissy had a history of run-ins with the law. Here he is seen upon his arrest in 1976 by the Clark County Sheriff's Department in Vancouver, Washington for a minor infraction.

After reading about Kathryn's murder, Molly Griggs, a close associate of Lissy's, notified police that the manner of Kathryn's death was similar to what Lissy had planned for a woman he didn't identify to her. Later, police found $300 in Molly's purse, the money Lissy had given her to leave town, but Griggs turned state's evidence instead and helped convict him.

Michael David Lissy was arrested and booked on the morning of October 13, 1984 by police investigative agents.

David Wilson, 31, originally agreed to "take the fall" for the murder for Lissy in return for $25,000, but confessed to stipulated facts about his role following Lissy's trial in return for life in prison.

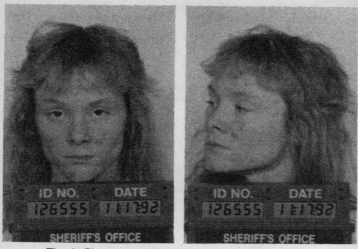

Tina LaPlante found David Wilson for Lissy to hire
to kill Kathryn.

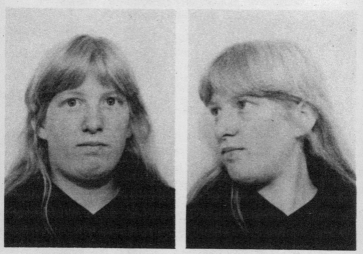

Gretchen Schumacher, Tina LaPlante's cousin, drove
Wilson to The Valley River Inn for $250 and later served as
one of the state's star witnesses.

While searching Lissy's van, police found the "hot" .357 magnum he bought for another hit man to kill his wife.

Detective David Poppe, now a sergeant, was one of the lead investigative agents with the Eugene Police Department.

Brian Barnes prosecuted the case as Lane County District Attorney. He is now in private practice.

J. Pat Horton supervised the prosecution of Lissy for the Lane County District Attorney's Office. He is now in private practice.

of June 1984, claiming that she no longer had adequate transportation to get back and forth to work. It was as good an excuse as any to separate herself from him, and happened to be the truth. She had figured, correctly, that he wouldn't want somebody working for him who may or may not show up on any given day due to transportation problems.

Nonetheless, it was apparent that Lissy continued to trust Beth and wanted to stay in touch with her. About three weeks before Kathy's murder, Lissy called her and asked her to meet him at Valley Scuba on Barbur Boulevard. He stressed that it was very important that she come, and she agreed. However, when she arrived driving a borrowed car, Lissy wasn't there.

She waited, and soon received a telephone call from Lissy that instructed her to meet him in downtown Portland at a restaurant. Beth again agreed, and this time Lissy was waiting at their prearranged location in the vicinity of Southwest Twelfth Avenue.

"He asked me at that time if I knew where to find a hot gun. I told him I didn't know. He kept asking about it, so I said, 'Okay, I'll look,' so he would quit bothering me about it. So very persistent a person. Then I called him later and told him I didn't know where he could find a hot gun."

A short time later Lissy contacted Beth again. This time he asked her if she knew where to find a hit man.

"I told him, 'No.' He said that there was somebody that had been following him, some Mexican person, and that is why he wanted the gun. He said that he had seen him following him around town. And he told me that he was afraid and that he needed this gun just in case, for protection. He said this person had called him and had made threats to him and was also threatening his family and friends. And that the man wanted ten thousand dollars. I didn't know why, you know, I couldn't imagine why anybody would just do that . . . I thought it was totally crazy . . . sounded like blackmail."

Lissy wouldn't take no for an answer, however, and persisted in his efforts to pressure Beth into finding him a hit man. A biker would do, he said.

"He asked if I knew any bikers," Beth said. "I said I didn't know any personally, but that he had some taking lessons from him at the scuba shop." She referred him to a scuba-diving student named Bill Kontz*, and Lissy told her that he would look into it himself.

"One other time I asked him, 'Well, did you find your hit man?' And he said, 'Yes.' And he told me not to say anything. That was the week before Kathy was murdered."

A week before that, Beth said, Lissy had called and asked her to clean the apartment across the street from the scuba shop.

"He said that he and Kathy were not getting along, and that he was going to leave her to stay at that apartment and that he wanted all of

Elise's things I imagine, put away upstairs in boxes and to clean the place up."

From that point on in the investigation, one person seemed to lead Davis and Poppe to another. Prostitutes and street people, many of whom, like Beth, were Lissy's own employees, helped the detectives fit the pieces of their homicide puzzle in place, each of which took them one step closer to nailing Lissy for his wife's murder.

One of those persons was Monica Glenn* another self-admitted prostitute, who told Davis and Poppe that Lissy had paid her to perform fellatio on him. Shortly before Kathy's death, Lissy had asked her to find him a hit man, just as he had asked Beth Cumley. Monica didn't know *who* Lissy wanted killed, but he had given her $240 as a down payment for the job. Monica told the detectives that she had made some contacts for Lissy, but the people she contacted just took Lissy's money with no intention of ever committing the crime. One person that she had contacted was David Atkinson.

Atkinson, the detectives learned, might have taken the job as Lissy's hit man had he not been arrested on June 29, 1984, for the Portland murder of Thomas Dougherty Kroder, twenty-three, a Dunkin' Donuts clerk and college student, the morning before. Kroder, working the graveyard shift at the Raleigh Hills shop, had just finished preparing a fresh batch of donuts when Atkinson, a junkie high on "speedballs," a combination of heroin and methamphetamine, walked in and blew Kroder's brains all over a back-room wall in a holdup of the donut shop. Kroder hadn't had a chance against the freaked-out Atkinson, who seemed just the type of person to commit Lissy's hit for him.

Monica told the detectives that Lissy gave her additional money on another occasion to acquire a gun for him. Lissy told her that he had already found someone to do the job, but he needed a gun. She told the detectives that she and her boyfriend "ripped off" the money without acquiring a gun for Lissy, and told Lissy that they had been "ripped off."

As the investigation into Kathryn Ann Martini-Lissy's murder entered its second month, Davis and Poppe felt that they were making good progress despite the fact that an arrest still lay somewhere in the future. Just how distant they had no way of knowing, but they were naturally anxious to sew things up. Their boss, Detective Sergeant Michael Cline, was on their backs because J. Pat Horton, the Lane County District Attorney, was on Cline's boss's back. Horton wanted enough evidence so that he could present the case to a grand jury which, he hoped, would hand down an indictment against Lissy.

The case moved forward in that direction when Davis and Poppe were led to Bary Franklin, a young black man who hung out on the streets of Portland. Franklin, they learned, had met Lissy for a variety of reasons that the detectives couldn't immediately clear up. But on one of those meetings in June, Franklin said, Lissy told him: "I have a job that I'd like you to do." According to what Franklin related to them, Lissy eventually told Franklin that he wanted somebody killed. He said that the victim would be his wife, and that she could be set up to be in a car at the proper moment. Lissy told Franklin that he would pay him one thousand dollars to kill her, and on his third meeting with Franklin, provided him with a .357 Colt and nine hundred dollars, one hundred dollars short of the agreed-upon amount.

Although Lissy didn't know it, Franklin really didn't think he would carry out the hit. Instead, he was planning to rip off Lissy for the money and the gun. But because of comments that Lissy had been making about other activities of a criminal nature, Franklin believed that Lissy was unstable and couldn't be trusted. As a result, he decided that he didn't want anything to do with the murder plot against Mrs. Lissy or the money. He met again with Lissy, returned the gun and the money, and told him that he was backing out of the deal. Lissy was furious. He said that he was desperate. Nonetheless, Franklin wanted nothing else to do with him and left Lissy with no choice but to continue looking for a killer. Franklin described the gun that Lissy had provided him with as having rubber grips and a two-and-a-half-inch barrel in a holster. When Davis and Poppe showed him the gun they had seized from Lissy's van, Franklin told them that it appeared to be the same gun.

During that second month of the investigation, Davis and Poppe again contacted Elise Dunn. She said that Lissy had been in touch with her at least twice, on August 9 and 10. She also wanted to tell them some things that Lissy had talked about prior to Kathy's death.

Elise reiterated how Lissy's desire for Kathy had stemmed from his intention to use her and her position at the bank to obtain a large loan and how, after he obtained the money, he planned to leave her and go back to Elise. She said that it was only after his attempts to use her banking connections had failed that Lissy decided to marry Kathy. His scheme, which required him to be married to Kathy, involved using Kathy's wealthy father for a substantial loan after they were married. She may have just been naive, reflected the cops, but those close to her had told them that she apparently had loved Michael Lissy. She had truly believed that he loved her, too, which made him all the more a scumbag in the detectives' eyes.

Elise told the detectives that Lissy had indicated a few weeks before Kathy's death that he had intended to get rid of Kathy so that he could go back to her. He described one scheme in which he planned to mix a stronger drug, which looked like cocaine, with some of the cocaine that he said Kathy used. Then when she sniffed it, thinking that it was cocaine, she would overdose and die. He had told her that he would give it to Kathy on one of her business trips when she was traveling to her bank's head office in Boston in June. When Kathy died, he would collect her insurance, a big insurance payday, because she would be out of town on business and the multiplier clause would be in effect. He had been very insistent that he would go back to Elise when he obtained the money.

But for reasons unknown to Elise, Lissy never went through with the plan. And as far as Davis and Poppe were concerned, talk of the plan may have simply been another of Lissy's lies. After all, they hadn't yet been able to substantiate Lissy's statements alleging Kathy's drug use.

Elise told Davis and Poppe that she had informed Lissy at one point, also before Kathy's death, that she no longer had any intention of going back to him. She said that she was living with the man that she would eventually marry, a man named Brad Lemmer*. When told of this, Lissy had begun to cry, she said, and told her, "Well, what if something happened to Kathy and Brad? Can we get back together then? What if they have an accident or something, can we get back together again?"

At various times during Lissy and Elise's later conversations, those in August after Kathy's death, Lissy had said that he was suspected by the police in Kathy's murder. He had informed Elise that his lawyer had told him that the police were building a good case around the circumstantial evidence, and once stated that she could hang him because of all the things that he had said to her including, of course, the statements in which he had said that he wanted to kill Kathy.

She told the investigators that Lissy, in August, after he knew that the cops were onto him, had offered to pay her a substantial amount of money for favorable testimony if the case ever went to court.

The investigation proceeded along in a similar fashion throughout the month of August, where Davis and Poppe continued to obtain bits and pieces of information but no hard-evidence that would fully implicate Lissy in Kathy's murder. But they now knew for certain that he was involved. The circumstantial evidence and the lies, along with their own gut feelings, told them so. But they still didn't know whether Lissy was the actual killer, or whether he had hired somebody to do it. There was evidence that pointed in both directions, but nothing so substantial that it would allow them to take the case to a grand jury or to bring actual charges

against Lissy. But they would get the evidence
they needed in due time. Of that they were certain.

Fifteen

On Friday, August 31, 1984, Robert McCorkle, a Eugene resident, was walking along a street near Hendricks Park in Eugene when he saw something that caught his eye in one of the lanes of traffic. It was an American Express credit card, lying next to a piece of white paper tissue. McCorkle walked out into the street and picked up the dusty, well-worn credit card, glanced at it, put it in his pocket, and continued on to his nearby destination, the Congregational church, where he worked in the counseling department.

After McCorkle finished his duties, he examined the credit card he'd found. He looked at the front and back sides, hoping to find a name so that he could return the card to its owner. However, he was unable to find the name. It had apparently been obliterated or somehow damaged so that it was no longer discernible. But there was an 800 number for American Express that remained readable. He called the number, to no avail. He was transferred to the offices of several different people, but got nowhere. Nobody would tell him who the card belonged to, nor would they suggest who he should contact about it.

Strangely, that same day Detective Edward Van Horn and Sergeant Michael Cline were called to the Stage Stop, a convenience market and gas station located on the corner of Sixth Avenue and Lincoln Street in Eugene. Someone, they were told by a store employee, had found some credit cards in one of the rest rooms. The cards bore the name Kathryn Martini-Lissy, so they didn't waste any time getting there. It was 3:50 P.M. when they arrived.

One of the cards was a Nordstrom credit card, another a Far West Daily Income Fund card, and the third a Far West Federal Savings check-guarantee card. The cards, they were told, had been found in the women's rest room that same day. The rest room had been cleaned earlier that morning, which meant that the cards had been left there sometime afterward. Van Horn and Cline seized the cards, placed them in appropriate evidence bags, and turned them over to Don Schuessler of their crime lab so that he could process them for fingerprints. It was doubtful, however, that any useful fingerprints could be obtained because of all the handling that had likely occurred prior to Van Horn and Cline's arrival.

Then on Sunday, September 2, McCorkle encountered one of his neighbors, Detective Wayne Irvin. McCorkle showed Irvin the card, told him where he'd found it, and explained how he had called American Express.

"I couldn't find out who it belonged to," McCorkle told Irvin. "They wouldn't help me in any way."

The next day Irvin turned in the card to his department and filed a brief report. Afterward, he recalled how Kathryn Martini-Lissy's credit cards had been reported missing by her husband, and he informed his colleagues, Davis and Poppe, about the card. By then they had all heard about the cards seized by Van Horn and Cline the previous Friday, the same day that McCorkle had found the American Express card. Together they checked the numbers on the card found by McCorkle against the numbers of Kathy's credit cards that had been provided by Michael Lissy. They discovered that the card matched one set of numbers. Another of Kathy's missing cards had been found.

Although the detectives tried to make something out of it all, nothing really came of it. It was all kind of strange, they felt. If they were wrong about Lissy, and they didn't believe they were, it could have been an indication that Kathy's killer was still in the Eugene area and had begun disposing of the items that he had taken from her room. On the other hand Lissy, or someone acting on his behalf, could have deposited the cards in public places as an attempt to throw the police off the track.

* * *

During the same time frame that Kathy's credit cards surfaced, the Eugene Police Department received a frantic telephone call from a young woman, Becky Norton*, who claimed to have been roughed up and raped by a "mad rapist" in a Eugene motel room. When the investigators contacted Norton and listened to her story, they thought about what had happened to Kathy at the Valley River Inn and naturally had to consider whether Becky was a victim of the man who had assaulted and murdered Kathy. Becky, whom the detectives considered a pretty flaky person, *seemed* pretty shaken up. But something in the back of their minds, call it a cop's instinct, warned them that she could be lying to them. Due to the nature of their jobs, however, they just couldn't dismiss her claims. Her claims had to be investigated, even if it meant that they would be chasing the wrong trail, even if it thrust them into an evil scheme that had already been set in motion weeks earlier.

Sixteen

At 1:50 P.M. on Thursday, September 13, 1984, Lissy appeared at the downtown Portland law offices of Kenneth Lee Baker and Michael Sturgeon. Lissy was there, voluntarily, to give a deposition to Robert A. Miller and Chris L. Mullmann, attorneys for the personal representative in Kathryn Ann Martini-Lissy's estate. Sturgeon, who was actually Lissy's attorney, couldn't be there and had asked his partner, Baker, to sit in for him. John J. Michelet, a notary public and court reporter, took down everything that was to go on the record.

Miller informed Lissy that he was going to ask him a number of questions regarding his and Kathy's personal effects. Specifically, he wanted to know the existence and location or whereabouts of certain assets. Lissy, instructed to respond verbally to their questions, said that he had moved out of the condominium that he and Kathy had shared several weeks earlier and was now staying with his friend, Al Blackman.

"Prior to that where were you living?" Miller asked.

"One twenty-eight Oswego Summit," Lissy responded.

"In Lake Oswego?"

"Correct."

"When you vacated those premises, did you lock up the condo?" Miller asked.

"Yes, I did," Lissy said.

"Have you been back since you left?"

"Yes, I have."

"On how many occasions?"

"Two, maybe three times."

"For what purposes?" Miller asked.

"To remove some personal effects," Lissy answered.

"Of yours or Kathy's?"

"Of mine."

"Are the personal effects of Kathy's still in the condominium?"

"Most of them are."

"Which ones are not?"

"Some of her clothing was removed," Lissy replied. "Her parents took quite a bit back with them, and I gave some to somebody else after they said it was okay before they left."

"After the Martinis said it was all right to give something to someone else?"

"Right."

"What was that?"

"They just said that—when they were out for the memorial service—'We have no objection to you giving her clothes to somebody who needs them or wants them.' "

"Was their permission or comment strictly limited to clothing?"

"No. They just—I believe Mr. Martini, you know, stated to me—I don't really recall if my father-in-law was present, but all he wanted out of the estate was the debt that Kathy owed him and the rest, you know, would go to me."

"All right. There are some items of personal property that were listed in the postnuptial agreement that you and Kathy executed some time ago. Can you tell me the whereabouts of Kathy's camera?"

"Hold on a second," Lissy said. The question seemed to catch Lissy off guard. He looked at his attorney, and asked to confer with him off the record. Lissy and Baker left the deposition room for a few moments. When they returned, Miller asked the question again.

"Where is Kathy's camera? Would you answer that question now?" Miller was insistent.

"I don't know," Lissy said. He shifted uneasily in his chair.

"Do you know which camera I am talking about?" Miller asked.

"Yes, I do."

"What kind of camera?"

"No, I don't even know the brand."

"Is it a one-hundred-thirty-five-millimeter type camera?"

"I think it is a thirty-five-millimeter."

"That's what I meant, thirty-five-millimeter,"

Miller said, becoming somewhat perturbed. "Did it come in a camera case with other lenses?"

"It has a little black case covering it."

"When is the last time you saw that camera?"

"I don't know. Kathy almost always had it with her."

"Even at work?"

"Yes. It was usually in the car with her."

"When is the last time you saw it?"

"I honestly can't recall."

"Do you know what its value was?"

"No."

"Did Kathy have that camera before you were married to her?"

"No, she did not."

"When did she purchase it?" Miller asked.

"When did she purchase it?" Lissy repeated, a puzzled look on his face. "She didn't. I gave it to her."

Lissy explained that he had given Kathy the camera sometime during the first two or three months that they were together, likely in July 1983. He told Miller and Mullmann that he had traded scuba equipment for the camera, but couldn't recall the brand or the person he had obtained it from. It seemed odd that Lissy's memory was keen on some points but so vague on others, but nobody said anything about it.

"Did you give Kathy any other gifts during your relationship with her?" Miller asked.

"I gave her a scuba outfit to use," Lissy replied.

"To use? Or was it hers?"

"It was hers."

"And by 'scuba outfit,' what do you mean by that?"

"Suit, tank, regulator, console, VC."

"Weight belt?"

"Weight belt."

"How about masks and things like that?"

"I honestly don't recall," Lissy said. "She had a lot of that because she had taken lessons before. It was fairly common practice for us to just, you know, keep upgrading equipment, just trade in the old one for a new one. . . ."

"All right. Let's go on to the other items of personal property that I am currently aware of. Her diamond necklace?"

"I don't know where that is at."

"When was the last time you saw it?"

"Probably the last time I saw Kathy."

"Did she wear it all the time?"

"Always."

"When is the last time you saw Kathy?"

"July fifth or sixth—July—"

"The day she was killed?"

"I don't know when she was killed," Lissy coolly said. "I am assuming it was Thursday. I believe it was July fifth."

"Was she wearing the necklace at that time?"

"To the best of my recollection, yes."

"What kind of necklace was it?"

"It had three little diamonds, kind of—each on the end of a little finger, kind of sprayed out." Lissy gestured with his hands.

"And it is something like a gold chain that people wear all the time?" Miller asked.

"It was on, like, a gold chain. I thought it was a gift to her from her dad because she, you know, she always wore it. But apparently it wasn't."

"She had it prior to your knowing her?"

"Correct."

"Do you remember what Kathy was wearing in terms of other jewelry on the last day that you saw her?"

"From actual physical observation, no. I know what she would tend to wear."

"Did she have a wedding ring?"

"I would believe she was wearing that."

"A wedding ring that you gave her?"

"Correct."

"Did it have a diamond in it?"

"I don't know if the wedding ring did. I believe it had a few chips in it. The engagement ring did have a diamond."

"Was it her practice to wear those all the time?"

"Yes."

"And where were those rings purchased?"

"I don't remember."

"Did you buy them?"

"We went down there together. I hate to shop, and after being in about ten jewelry stores she finally, you know, had to have that setup so she finally found it. I came down and we went to the place."

It seemed strange that he couldn't even remember where he purchased the rings. It had been such a short time ago. It was something that most men remembered, even years later, no matter whether they had shopped around for it or not. Getting married was such a big, happy event in most people's lives, and picking out and buying wedding sets should have been a memorable, not a matter-of-fact, event.

"Did you pay cash for it or write a check?" Miller asked.

"I don't recall."

"Do you recall if it was money from her account, from your account, or from a joint account?"

"It was—it was probably cash from me and a check on her part."

"Did you have a checking account at that time?"

"I don't really recall."

"Do you remember when you purchased it?"

"No, I don't."

"Was it within a month of your wedding?"

"Oh, no. It was much before that."

"When did you become engaged?"

"I believe in August of eighty-three."

"Would you have purchased it to give to her as an engagement gift as far as the engagement ring was concerned?"

"No. I got it after we became engaged."

"So it would be between August and January some time?"

"Correct."

"Because you were married, January what?"

"Twenty-eighth."

"Of eighty-four?"

"Yes."

"Do you know if she had the ring on when she was in Eugene?"

"I would assume so."

"How about other jewelry? Did she wear her Yale class ring?"

"I don't believe so."

"Do you know where that is?"

"No, I don't."

"When is the last time you saw that?"

"I can't actually recollect ever seeing that, but it may be at the condo."

"Did she have a jewelry box she kept her jewelry in?"

"Yes."

"Where is that?"

"At the condo."

"Do you have a key to the condo?"

"I believe I do."

"Do you have it with you today?"

"No, I don't."

"Do you have it readily accessible so we could get it today?"

"Why would you want it?"

"Because I want to inventory personal effects in the condominium today."

Lissy shifted uneasily again, and fidgeted with his hands. He looked at his attorney.

"We will give it to you," Baker offered. "I don't know about it. I don't know where it is or the circumstances. Nobody requested ahead of time to have the key. We certainly would have provided it if they had."

"Well, where is the key today?" Miller asked Lissy. It was very clear that he wanted an answer.

"I don't know, truthfully," Lissy answered. "I tried to go in yesterday and we thought that the locks had been changed."

"Who is the manager of the condominium?"

"I don't know."

"You were not on the condominium title, were you?"

"I believe not."

"Do you have any personal knowledge as to whether or not the manager of those condominiums even knew you lived there?"

"I don't have that personal knowledge."

"Did you ever meet him—or her?"

"I met a lot of people that were there. I don't know who does what there."

"So you don't even know the manager's name?"

"No."

"Would the key to the condominium be at your place of residence now?"

"That is a possibility."

"When is the last time you were in there, 'there' being the condominium?"

"Over a month ago."

"Did you use a key to get in?"

"Yes."

"Is it on a key ring?"

"Yes."

"What does that key ring look like?"

"Just a silver standard key ring."

"With more than one key?"

"Yes. I believe there's a couple car keys on it."

"Where is the office for the manager?"

"Right in the complex."

"Is it marked 'Manager' or something like that?"

"Well, there is a fountain and you just drive right up from there. It is kind of in a central position. . . . I quite honestly tried to get in yesterday to get some coats for myself but the two keys I tried didn't fit."

"Do you have a key to the mailbox?" Miller asked.

"No, but the lock has been removed."

"So what do you mean, the lock has been removed?"

"They took it out, the Postal Service."

"So do you have—do you have access to what is in there?"

"Well, I can get the mail because they are not putting it in the box."

"What are they doing with it?"

"Just putting it in the office."

Minutes earlier Lissy had said that he didn't know the manager of the condominium complex, yet in practically the next breath he told Miller and Mullmann that he had begun picking up the mail from the office. It didn't seem likely that he could *not* know the manager if he was allowed to pick up the mail from the office. Couldn't this guy tell the truth about *anything*?

"Do you have the mail?"

"Yes."

"Up through yesterday?"

"Yeah."

"Did you bring any of that with you today?"

"What I have of it."

Lissy explained that he had been throwing out all of the magazines and junk mail, but had brought what he thought was important. He also said that he didn't think he had instructed the Postal Service to remove the lock from the mailbox and to start delivering it to the office. He said that the mail carrier had apparently done that on her own, though he had inquired about getting access to the mail. He said he was told he'd have to make arrangements with the condominium office.

As Lissy's deposition continued on into the afternoon of September 13, he appeared to become more nervous and flustered at Miller's questioning. Judging by some of Lissy's responses, it sometimes appeared that he felt like his integrity was being impugned by the questioner's tone. Of course it was all a part of his facade because, as could be seen from his past acts of lies and deceit, he had little, if any, in-

tegrity to impugn. But it was necessary for him
to keep up the act. To do otherwise at this point
would bring his world down, utterly destroy
what he had worked so hard to achieve.

"Did you give any other property of Kathy's
away to anyone?" Miller asked.

"I believe not," Lissy answered smugly.

"Do you think that if you would have, you
would remember here today?"

"If I could—that's a rather dumb question,"
Lissy said, showing his anger. "If I could remember I would tell you. I just don't. I don't
believe I did (give anything else away)."

"Have you kept most of her financial records?"

"Pretty much so, yes. I have just thrown out
junk mail that came in, advertisements and
things like that."

"Do you know if Kathy had any stocks or
bonds?"

"I really—there appears to be some from some
of the information that has come in, but I don't
understand most of it."

"Can you explain that answer? You said something that has come in makes it appear to be
that she has some stocks?"

"There's some things that have come in that
look like stocks and things like that. I never really—"

"Dividends?"

"I don't know. I don't know how to read those
things."

"Did Kathy ever talk to you about her stock portfolio?"

"The only thing she—when we first got together she had some stock or something, or had some stocks from a friend of hers, and she sold that. I don't even recall the reasons now."

When asked if he had paid any of Kathy's personal bills after her death, such as her American Express account, car payment, condominium payment, car- and condo-insurance premiums, and so forth, Lissy responded that he had not. He appeared to be getting more perturbed at the line of questioning, and let it be known to those present.

"I am going to make a brief statement," Lissy said. "I honestly don't know what bills were paid and who got what and that sort of thing. I never handled those. We had a joint-checking account, and after a while, since I never wrote checks on it, she closed it out. I don't know how many different policies she has had. I have tried to make some heads or tails out of them but it doesn't—I don't know who got paid what. It just, you know, in hindsight, yes, I should have known but I never have bothered with things like that."

"How about the title or registration to her car? Do you know where that was?" Miller wasn't giving an inch.

"No. I would assume it was in the car."

"She had a Datsun, didn't she? Brand-new?"

"Sure."

"What, a three-hundred?"

"Three-hundred."

"Did she take that to Eugene with her on business?"

"Yes."

"How did it get back from Eugene?"

"A friend of mine, the person I am staying with, drove it back."

"What did he do with it when he brought it back?"

"Put it in the garage."

"At the condominium?"

"Correct."

"Did you know if it was paid for or not?"

"I knew that we were making some sort of payment on it."

"And your name was not on that car?"

"I believe not."

"Did Kathy have any allowance from her employer for her car purchase?"

"I believe so."

"Was that paid directly to her in cash?"

"I don't know."

"You said you had a joint-checking account and she closed that. Where was that joint-checking account?"

"I—I really don't know. I believe it was at Far West Federal, because that's where most of her business was because they gave her the condo loan."

In response to Miller's probing for answers, Lissy said that Kathy had an IRA at her bank, but that he didn't know whether she had a pension or a profit-sharing account through her employer. He also said that he didn't believe that she owned any other real property, nor any mobile homes, boats, or recreational vehicles of which he was aware. Throughout much of the proceeding, Lissy's responses seemed vague, and at times evasive. On other points in which the facts were known to others, particularly information about Kathy's life-insurance policies, Lissy's answers were direct and to the point. It became obvious that he knew much more about Kathy's personal life than he was admitting, but divulged information only when he had no other choice.

Seventeen

By the time Michael David Lissy was giving his deposition to the attorneys representing Kathy's estate, Detectives Lloyd Davis and David Poppe had made considerable progress in their investigation, mainly through their continued contact with a number of street people in Portland. As a result, they were now looking for a man named David Wilson, thirty-one, whom they now had reason to believe was involved in Kathy's murder, possibly as a hit man hired by Lissy.

Wilson's name had come up when Davis and Poppe learned about and contacted Gretchen Marie Schumacher, twenty, a tough-looking, tough-talking, woman, aged beyond her years due to her lifestyle. Gretchen, they were told, had acted as a "pimp" for Lissy on occasion by soliciting "dates" for him with young prostitutes in exchange for a fee. When they checked out Gretchen with the Portland Police Bureau, Davis and Poppe learned that she had been associated with a subject who had been arrested for soliciting customers for prostitutes. Although they hadn't obtained information that Gretchen herself performed sexual acts for money, Davis and Poppe soon learned from Stephanie Malone*, nineteen, who went by the street name "Starbuck," that Gretchen was a lesbian. Starbuck herself was a self-admitting bisexual who leaned toward lesbianism and that, she said, was how she knew about Gretchen's homosexual tendencies.

During one of their first interviews with Gretchen, she admitted to setting up dates with prostitutes for Lissy. She also told the detectives that she had set up a fifteen–year-old hooker for Lissy and remarked that she was "into child molesting" herself. Gretchen told them that one of the dates she set up for Lissy had occurred one week after Kathy's death. Gretchen at first denied any involvement in the death of Lissy's wife, and denied knowing David Wilson.

As a result, Davis and Poppe returned to Starbuck for more information. Under pressure of being called before a grand jury and possibly indicted on some charge related to the case, Starbuck reluctantly told them that both Gretchen and David Wilson had told her that they had driven to Eugene in the car of Gretchen's cousin, Tina LaPlante, a 1973 Oldsmobile, and had killed Lissy's wife.

According to Starbuck, Gretchen knew Kathy's room number at the Valley River Inn. Gretchen and David Wilson had apparently told Starbuck that Gretchen had gained entry into Kathy's room, and that she, Gretchen, had let David Wilson into the room a short time later. Gretchen then returned to the car, leaving David Wilson to kill Kathy. Of course Davis and Poppe didn't know how much of Starbuck's story was fact or fiction. Sometimes stories had a way of changing as they were passed along from one person to the next. But they were determined to put it all together and learn the truth.

Gretchen purportedly told Starbuck that she and Wilson had been instructed to take property from the victim to make the murder appear to be motivated by robbery. Wilson, however, took more of Kathy's "things" than he was supposed to, which had angered Gretchen. Gretchen told Starbuck that Wilson had told her that he had taken Kathy's property as "collateral" in case Lissy did not pay them as he had promised. Gretchen also told Starbuck that she was upset with Wilson because he had not taken Kathy's $6,000 wedding ring off her body after the killing. It didn't take Davis and Poppe very long to decide that these were some pretty cold-blooded people with whom they were dealing, people who obviously held very little value for human life, unless it was their own. Starbuck's sister, Melanie Malone*, who went by the street name "Peaches," provided the detectives with a similar version of events related to Kathy's murder.

Larry Wingate*, who was having sexual liaisons with Starbuck, told the detectives about a "confession" Gretchen had made that implicated Gretchen and Wilson in Kathy's murder.

Unfortunately, Wingate couldn't, or perhaps chose not to, recall the specifics of the conversation.

However, Rita Wingate*, Larry Wingate's fifteen–year-old daughter, told the detectives that she had given Lissy blow jobs in return for money during dates that had been set up by Gretchen Schumacher. She also told them that Gretchen had told her that Gretchen and Wilson had committed Kathy's murder. She also said that Gretchen had told her that she and Wilson had taken a checkbook, credit cards, and other property belonging to Kathy at the time of the murder.

Interestingly, Davis and Poppe learned that Rita Wingate was taken from her father's home by the state Children's Services Division and placed in the home of Gretchen's parents because Rita's father allegedly had been sexually abusing her.

Tina Rula LaPlante, nineteen, had recently given birth to a child at Emanuel Hospital in Portland on September 4, 1984. Tina, another self-admitting Portland prostitute, first met Lissy during the summer of 1983. She had worked for him, and Davis and Poppe turned up information which indicated that she was also involved sexually with Lissy in return for money, in addition to working on the streets of Portland as a prostitute. By the time Davis and Poppe had tracked her down, Tina had heard that she had been implicated in Kathy's murder and was naturally pretty shaken up. At first she wouldn't talk to the detectives, and they had to piece the story together from the statements that they had already obtained from others.

Three months before giving birth to her child, during her second trimester, Tina had gone on a "date" with Lissy at the apartment on Barbur Boulevard. It was during this sexual encounter that Lissy told her he was looking for somebody to commit a killing for him. He asked Tina if she knew somebody who would do it for him. He said that he wanted a lady killed and probably raped, and that he wanted her strangled or hit over the head. He told her that he wanted both the woman and Elise Dunn's boyfriend killed, and indicated that he would pay $10,000 for the job. He told Tina that he would give her $500 if she introduced him to somebody, and she had assured him that she would look into it for him.

After the sexual encounter with Lissy, Tina went to the home of Linda Crewes*, a house that was known in the drug underworld as the "Tweak House," *tweak* being a slang term for the feeling a person gets when injecting and/or snorting speed or methamphetamine. The Tweak House was frequented by Tina, Starbuck, Peaches, David Wilson, and a number of other people who abused illicit drugs. While there Tina asked if anyone knew anybody who would kill somebody for $10,000. David Wilson, who was taking drugs with the others, told her that he would do it.

According to the story that the detectives were being told, Tina telephoned Lissy and arranged a meeting between him and Wilson. Soon thereafter, Tina and Wilson met with Lissy again, at which time Lissy gave Wilson an as yet undetermined amount of money so that he could get a haircut, buy a suit, and obtain a rental car. The person to be killed, he had told them, was out of town in a motel and Lissy wanted Wilson to look respectable so that he would fit in with the environment. Lissy told Wilson that he "wanted a rape," and said that the murder had to be done by 8 P.M. on July 5. He said the lady would be expecting somebody named "Steve."

Davis and Poppe soon learned that David Wilson lived with his mother in a nearly dilapidated, single-story unpainted wood-frame house. Wilson's residence was located a fifth of a mile off Alvord Road in Beaverton, Oregon, along Route 1, the first house on the left of a long, dusty, unpaved and unnamed road.

Surrounded by tall Douglas fir trees on all sides, the run-down house had an old, broken-down school bus parked on one side of the drive, alongside several useless tires and a couple of cords of firewood. Along the other side of the road were several old junked cars, which made the place look like a wrecking yard.

When the detectives knocked on the door, they were informed by Wilson's mother that Wilson did indeed live there, but he was not at home at that time.

Back in Portland, Davis and Poppe asked their colleagues to run a check on Wilson. When they did, they turned up an unrelated arrest from 1983 and produced a mug shot of him for the detectives. When Davis and Poppe looked at Wilson's photo they were astounded when they realized that Lissy and Wilson were practically "doubles" of each other. When they laid down the mug shot of Wilson alongside a mug shot of Lissy that was taken in Clark County, Washington, a few years before, they noted that the resemblance was uncanny. They decided that Bonita Jean Golliher, the night maintenance supervisor at the Valley River Inn, may have been mistaken when she had identified Lissy as having been there on the night of the killing. They showed the pictures of Lissy and Wilson to several people who had no connection to the case. Those people in turn told them that they were showing them photographs of the same individual. As a result, Davis and Poppe now believed that Golliher had seen Wilson, not Lissy, on the night of the killing. That theory added credence to the stories that they had been receiving in which Lissy had hired Tina, Gretchen, and Wilson to kill his wife. He hadn't done it himself, as they had begun to believe for a while. In keeping with his past patterns, Lissy had again found someone else to do his dirty work for him.

In an effort to shake things up, it was decided to present the facts of the case to a Lane County grand jury on September 25, 1984. Two weeks earlier, Davis and Poppe served subpoenas on Michael Lissy, Rita Wingate, Larry Wingate, Gretchen Schumacher, David Wilson, Stephanie Malone, Melanie Malone, Linda Crewes, Tina LaPlante, and others. Each were advised that their appearances were mandatory, and if they failed to appear a warrant would be issued for their arrest.

Tina didn't show up. Instead she called from a point along Interstate 5 and told the detectives that her 1973 Oldsmobile had broken down. Davis and Poppe tried to impress upon her that if she didn't come clean with what she knew about Lissy's involvement in Kathy's murder, she would do hard jail time right along with Lissy and Wilson.

The grand jury, meanwhile, didn't get much out of the others. Although some evidence was taken during the proceedings, including testimony, hair samples, fingerprints, handwriting samples, anything that might fit in and help make the case, indictments weren't yet handed down. It was determined that Lissy's fingerprints were found on one of the fifty-dollar bills that he had given Molly Griggs, and some of Wilson's head and pubic hairs were determined to be microscopically similar to those found inside Kathy's hotel room. But it still wasn't enough to make arrests. They needed something more, something conclusive. All the grand-jury proceedings really accomplished at that point was to shake things up, causing a lot of conversation among the witnesses. But the controversy helped the district attorney's office tighten its net around Lissy.

Tina LaPlante was served another subpoena to return to grand jury the following week. Her lawyer subsequently contacted the Lane County District Attorney's office and worked out an agreement that if Tina had valuable information, she would share it in return for immunity from prosecution. It was agreed that she could have been a participant in the planning or the passing of money, or an accessory of some type, and still receive immunity as long as she hadn't been physically present when the murder was committed. If evidence surfaced that she had been present, or if she had lied about anything, all bets were off.

Tina, at Davis's and Poppe's urging, agreed to call Lissy in an attempt to obtain his statement of his involvement in Kathy's murder. Tina also, although more reluctantly, agreed to wear a bodywire transmitting device in an attempt to obtain a confession to Kathy's murder from Wilson.

Eighteen

Tina LaPlante fancied herself a gangster of sorts. A bubbly girl with a lot of guts, she ran with a rough and bawdy crowd, and that's precisely how she became mixed up with the likes of Michael David Lissy. It turned out that Tina knew a lot about Lissy's plans to kill his wife, much more than Detectives Lloyd Davis and David Poppe had initially suspected.

It turned out that not only did she know about the murder plans, but Davis and Poppe confirmed that she had been another of the many persons that Lissy had solicited to find him a killer. She had been one of the persons that Lissy thought he could trust, someone he thought would lie if questioned by the police. Moreover, Lissy felt that nobody would believe any of these street people anyway, if they did in fact decide to talk and tell the truth. That had been the theory, at least, that Lissy had operated under when he contacted Tina and all of the others. The fact that he had been wrong was the theory that Davis and Poppe operated under when they enlisted

Tina's help and urged the district attorney to make a deal with her.

During that same time frame Gretchen Schumacher, frightened by the grand-jury proceedings, had apparently left the state. Although the police couldn't locate her, Tina seemed to have some information about her sudden departure. But she told the cops that she didn't know where Gretchen had fled. If she did know where Gretchen was hiding out, she wasn't going to say. At least not yet. Because they didn't need Gretchen just yet, the detectives didn't push the issue and put the subject of her disappearance aside for the moment so that they could focus their attention on Lissy and Wilson.

Since Tina knew about Lissy's plots and subplots, it seemed very natural for her to be the one to approach Lissy and bring up certain subjects related to Kathy's murder. But because Lissy had been cautious and had patted her down on prior meetings, everyone agreed that it wouldn't be a good idea to put a body wire on her because of its bulk. The body wire would probably be okay to use when she met with Wilson, but not Lissy. Lissy, if he chose to pat her down again, would be able to feel the tape recorder and equipment on her body. To play it even safer, it was decided that she would call him on the telephone instead of going to a face-to-face meeting with him.

* * *

On Monday, October 8, 1984, shortly after 3 P.M., Davis and Poppe brought Tina to the Portland Police Bureau for the purpose of calling Lissy at his parents' home on the Oregon coast where he was now living. Acting under court order, the telephone call was tape recorded. Davis dialed the number, and a half minute or so later Ernest Lissy, Michael's father, answered.

"Hello," Ernest said.

"Is Michael there?" Tina asked.

"No, he isn't. Who's this?"

"This is Tina. Do you know when he's going to be back?"

"Yeah, well he's just up doing a job in Lincoln City for me, doing a little work. This is his dad. Can I help you?"

"Well, will you just tell him that Tina's trying to get ahold of him?"

"Yeah, Tina. You can tell me anything there is to say because I can pass the word to him. I mean we know all about everything, so if there is anything you wanta tell me, why, don't be afraid to tell me. I'm his dad."

"What'd he tell you?" Tina asked, somewhat startled by Ernest's sudden probing.

"Well, about his situation. About the fact, you know, with the Eugene Police and all that."

"He told you the truth?" Tina asked.

"What is the truth?" Ernest seemed interested in learning as much as he could from her.

"Well, just tell him I'm trying to get a hold of him."

"Okay, how does he get a hold of you?" Ernest asked.

"Just tell him to call my aunt's. I can try to call back. When's he gonna be there?"

"Well, it wasn't going to be a very long job. Let's see, the trouble is I took off and I don't know what time they left, but I would guess, if you called back by, let's see, how about 4:30?"

"Uh, listen, I think I hear a noise out there. Let me check and see if he just came in."

"Oh, you think he pulled up?"

"Just hang on, okay?"

A few more seconds ticked by, and Tina could hear Ernest Lissy telling his wife, Patricia, to go outside and tell Michael to hurry up and get to the telephone. A few seconds later, Michael Lissy came on the line.

"Hello," Lissy said.

"Michael?"

"Yeah."

"Hi."

"How you doin'?" Lissy asked when he recognized Tina's voice.

"Fine. How are you doin'?"

"Oh, goin' crazy."

"Yeah, I bet."

"Did you go down to the grand jury?" he asked.

"No, I got a lawyer and pleaded the fifth," Tina said. "So I didn't even have to go. Can you talk on your phone?"

"Well, I don't think it'd be cool."

"Your parents are right there?"

"Well, yeah. But they're (the phones) probably tapped."

"Do you want to go to a phone booth and call me?"

"Uh, yeah, I could."

"How long will it take you?"

"Oh, five minutes."

"Okay, do that." She gave him the number.

"Okay." Lissy repeated the number to her to make sure he had copied it down correctly.

"Okay. Hurry," Tina urged.

Tina had told the detectives about yet another scheme Lissy had devised. Because of all the heat from the Eugene and Portland police and Lissy's burning desire to get his hands on the insurance money, Lissy had developed a plan in which he had encouraged David Wilson to turn himself in, to admit that he, alone, was responsible for killing Kathy. He wanted Wilson to tell the police that he had a drug connection with Kathy, lost his head, and killed her in the heat of the moment, during the heat of passion. Wilson was supposed to say that drugs had clouded his mind. Lissy insisted that if Wilson did as he was told, he would get off on manslaughter instead of being convicted of aggravated murder, and that he would do perhaps three to five years in prison. If Wilson would stick to that story and do the time, Lissy had promised that he would pay Wilson $25,000, upon his release from prison. According to Lissy's plan, everybody would end up happy. The police would have their killer, and Lissy would have his freedom and would collect the insurance money. Lissy was quick to point out to Wilson that he couldn't collect the insurance money if it was proven that he was responsible for his wife's death.

Born and raised in poverty with a life lived mostly on the streets, $25,000 was a lot of money in David Wilson's mind. Wilson initially agreed to take the rap for Lissy, since he figured he was going to do some jail time anyway. After all, the cops seemed to be getting pretty close. And the grand-jury proceedings had frightened Wilson, probably more than it had frightened Gretchen. He didn't want to do life in prison, and somehow three to five years seemed tolerable.

Several minutes later Lissy called the number that Tina had given him. There was hope yet that she could get him to say something incriminating. Cagey, Lissy played word games with Tina at first.

"Howdy," Lissy said when Tina picked up the phone.

"Hi. Do your parents know anything?"

"No. They just know what I told them," Lissy said.

"You know, I didn't do anything," Lissy said.

"Huh? There's a lot of static on the phone." Tina couldn't believe Lissy's denial about his involvement, especially to *her*.

"Yeah. It's common down here."

"So, did you go to the grand jury?" Tina asked.

"Yeah."

"What'd they say?"

"Well, they had me take the fifth, and then they took hair samples," Lissy said.

"Really."

"And handwriting samples, and a picture."

"And you didn't have to say nothin'?"

"No."

"You know Dave still wants to do that?"

"Yeah." Lissy responded affirmatively to Tina's question about Wilson taking the fall for him, and Davis and Poppe were quick to make note of it.

"He told me he needs five hundred bucks," Tina said. "So he can, you know, party or whatever before he goes, you know."

"I just don't have it."

"That's what I told him, and he says well, 'Then maybe I should just take off.' But then you know what would happen. Me and you would, you know."

"There's nothin' I can do."

"Listen, I can tell him you can't get no money, right?"

"Yeah."

"Okay, cause you know he doesn't wanta get aggravated murder . . . right? He'd rather get manslaughter."

"Yeah."

"So how would the connection between him and Kathy be?" Tina asked, trying to get Lissy to lay out the scenario regarding Wilson taking the fall.

"Bad, you know. He heard that we had a lot of money and he knew she was buying dope, you know, and that's, he went down to try . . . he could say he had been sellin' her cocaine for awhile, you know, for six months," Lissy said, laying out the plan that he wanted Wilson to follow.

"That's what I suggested."

"But if he does do it, no matter what, he has to hold the line."

"He's got to make 'em believe that you didn't set it up," Tina said.

"Yeah. No matter what they threaten with or say who said what, you know. Somebody had to have said something for them to have gotten so close."

"Somebody what?"

"Well, my lawyer said on those hair samples that they should have known within the hour whose they were. They were testin' me, too, like they think maybe I did it."

"Huh?"

"You know, it might have all been just fishing," Lissy said. "I don't know whether the grand jury's still going on or not . . . I wish Gretchen hadn't run, that looks bad."

"Yeah, it does."

"I don't know if they have her. They could be holding her."

"I don't know," Tina said. "All I know is he's got to make his story stick."

"Well, what's he gonna do? Wait until they pick him up?"

"No. I think he was gonna turn himself in."

"Okay. Just tell him to hold because they'll threaten him with everything. Now be careful they're not watching you guys when you're meeting."

"Yeah, I know."

"The best thing (story) would be is that he'd seen us both (Kathy and Lissy) with lots of cash and for some reason that night he just went crazy and, you know, jumped her."

Lissy again suggested that Wilson tell the police that he had been selling cocaine to Kathy for six months or more, and to stress that she had connections in Eugene. Tina also mentioned that she was supposed to have sex with Wilson as part of the deal involving him taking the fall for Lissy.

"Well, I'm surprised they haven't come and picked us up yet," Lissy said. "What does your lawyer tell you?"

"He's just tellin' me to plead the fifth until they get evidence that I'm withholding evidence."

"Yeah. Well, they might have somebody . . . who told them something. Maybe it was Starbuck."

"What did you tell Starbuck?" Tina asked.

"Nothing. I think Starbuck read something in the paper or somebody told her something and she tried to put things together, and she probably sold it to the police for some sort of deal. Yeah, and I think that's why they're tryin' to nail you."

"Yeah. They're getting to me bad."

"Well, again, no matter what they say or do, you hold. And I'm holding. And we just have to hope Gretchen does. Have you seen or heard from her?"

"Nope. I'm wondering about her."

"They might have her down there and are holding her. But if she'd have said anything, we'd all be in trouble. Are you at a pay phone?"

"Yeah. I'm downstairs at Meier and Frank's," Tina said. Meier and Frank is a downtown Portland department store, and there are pay telephones in the basement level.

"I'll tell you what," Lissy said, getting cagey again. "If you need to call me again, when you give me your number, add ten to the final digit. Like if it's thirty-nine, say forty-nine. That way if I call you back, they can't get at either line."

"Yeah."

"So just add ten to it, so thirty-nine becomes forty-nine."

"Okay. Have you heard anything about your insurance money?"

"I won't hear anything until they solve the murder."

"Until he goes?"

"Yeah. Then it'll probably be ninety days to six months. They're gonna grill him like hell. They're gonna try to prove it. And he's gotta deny it all the way along. And they may threaten him with first degree and conspiracy and all that sort of thing. But if he sticks to his story, there's nothin' they can do . . . And you gotta stick, I gotta stick, and Gretchen's gotta stick."

"Yeah. You know me. Shit."

"Yeah."

"You know what?" Tina continued. "I won't even meet him (Wilson). I'm scared to meet him. I don't think he just wants to go to bed with me. What do you think?"

"I think he does. I think he wants you to tell him you love him and you will forever be his."

"I think he just wants to get rid of me."

"I don't think so. Wouldn't do him any good."

"Yeah, it would," Tina insisted. "Because then there's no connection."

"Well, do what you think's best. The thing is, if they had anything on him, he'd be in jail."

"Could be," Tina said. "Or maybe they just need more evidence."

"The sooner Dave goes in, the sooner I get the money," Lissy said. "What I'll do for him is put it all in savings bonds."

"He said he doesn't want me to even pick it up until after a year goes by."

"I agree. And what I'll do is start taking it out in savings bonds so he'll actually have twenty-five plus whatever interest."

"You know. I shouldn't have even got him to do this. He runs around, telling people different things."

"Well, that's good, though. He's told a lot of people a lot of different stories, so they might believe him. If he says, 'I did it, I didn't take any money for it,' they have to take him at that."

"Have you told anybody at all?" Tina asked.

"No, not a soul. I wouldn't, you know. And I don't care what goes down. I'm sayin' I'm innocent."

"What about Gretchen? I think Gretchen might have said some things."

"Just a . . . hophead . . . See, Dave ought to get a lawyer and turn himself in. Plea-bargain for what he can get. And tell him not to take any deals (implicating Lissy) or anything like that, or there's no money. Okay? Just tell him to get the best deal for himself. They'll probably let him have either manslaughter or just regular murder, and he can be out in five years, if he, you know, (does) good behavior."

"Yeah."

"So, I don't think Gretchen said anything or we'd all be had, because then they'd have an eyewitness," Lissy said.

They made small talk for a while, discussed the weather, and Lissy finally commented that he thought that Starbuck was the one feeding information to the police. Davis and Poppe couldn't have been happier. It was clear that

Lissy wasn't suspicious of Tina. If he was, he wouldn't have talked so much.

"You know, my parents appreciate how nice you've been to me," Lissy said. "I told them what a friend you are, how you've helped me try to find the killer, and that the police have been harassing you for it."

"Yeah, man. I was worried about that, Michael."

"Well, they were trying to scare you. Somebody has said something. Obviously it's not enough or we'd all be in jail. It's probably just the street hearsay."

"How come the cops are asking about credit cards?"

"Well, I don't know what Dave took out of the room."

"Yeah."

"Do you know what she had there?" Tina was getting bold, but she had already developed the rapport between her and Lissy, set the pace, so there was little chance of scaring him off now. She had to try, and was by now beginning to enjoy it a little.

"Well, credit cards, money," Lissy said.

"And they're talkin' about jewelry."

"Huh?"

"They're talkin' about jewelry, too."

"Well, that's a possibility, too. You know I think he ought to get himself a lawyer and work out the best deal he can."

"He said he can do it. He's gotta know how they met, or whatever."

"Might say that Gretchen introduced them," Lissy suggested. He thought about his last statement for a few seconds, then added: "Well, we better not."

Lissy suggested that Tina prompt Wilson to tell the police that he had met Kathy through another person, that he should just make up a man's name, and that his purpose for meeting her was to sell her cocaine. It was about the third or fourth time that Lissy had worked out a variation on the scenario.

"You know what? He probably wants me to get the five hundred bucks so he can just take off," Tina said. "Then what do you think will happen?"

"I don't think we should talk anymore in case they're setting up a tap," Lissy said. He was either becoming paranoid or suspicious. It was difficult to tell which.

"Well, we gotta talk, you know," Tina insisted.

"Just tell him I've got no money . . . without him there's no case."

"Yeah."

"Now they could pick us up any time, 'cause the grand jury could be getting done any day. So if you have a way of reaching him that's safe, I'd just tell him he's gotta get a lawyer and work out the best deal he can."

"Okay, I'll tell him the story."

"If I don't move on the insurance within the

next week or so, I may lose it anyway. Her parents are suing me, and as long as the case is settin' out there, nothin' happens. They think somebody probably gave [the cops] a tip. They were dead for a while, then somebody probably gave them a tip."

"You know, the cops probably think that you were there because you look a lot like Dave."

"Yeah, I've thought about that a lot. But if somebody identifies me now, I've put on forty pounds since Kathy died, my hair is a lot longer, my beard's scraggly. It's just cause I haven't had the money even for a haircut. And of course I've been so upset, I've just been eating like a pig."

"You're not feeling bad about it, are you?" Tina asked.

"No. Are you?"

"No. Not yet."

"Believe me, I will not break. Okay?"

"All right."

"I don't care if I have to go to trial and everything else, I will not break. They can't offer me any type of deal because there ain't no deal they can offer me. You know, they might say manslaughter. Bullshit. Five years in jail might as well be five hundred to me."

Tina agreed.

"We may get arrested in the next couple of days," Lissy continued. "But if he goes ahead and does his thing, he'll have twenty-five plus interest in there if he's in three years, which is what he'll probably get."

"If you ever want another of your wives killed, don't ask me, okay?"

"I won't," Lissy said. "I will never even think of another thing."

Tina hung up.

The case was finally coming together.

Nineteen

By now Davis and Poppe had more than ample reason to focus on David Wilson as Kathy's killer. They had talked to Melanie Malone, again, and she told them that Wilson had made incriminating statements to her about Kathy's murder, statements that only the killer and the police could know, such as the ashtray on the bed near Kathy's body. They wanted to nail Wilson quickly, but they lacked the hard physical evidence they needed to make the charges stick in court. They couldn't just arrest him based on the circumstantial evidence and hearsay that they had, and they couldn't rely on the possibility that he might walk in at any time and admit his involvement. He could just as easily run. No, they knew that they had to have something more, and that's where Tina would come in again.

But first they contacted Ben Brown*, another informant from Portland's underworld. Under questioning, Brown told Davis and Poppe that he and Wilson had become friends, but Brown had become disturbed by what Wilson had only recently told him. Wilson had essentially admitted to Brown that he had killed Kathy Martini-Lissy at the Valley River Inn. Brown, unnerved over the confession and upset that he'd been so easily drawn in by Wilson, told the detectives that he would be willing to wear a body wire to get Wilson's confession for them. Wilson trusted him, he said, and he felt that he could get him to talk about the murder again. Despite the offer, however, the detectives decided that they would try Tina first. Wilson seemed to have a romantic interest in her, and that might be enough to get him to go into more detail when she got him to talk.

As much to find and seize evidence as to shake things up even more, Davis and Poppe served search warrants on David Wilson's home in Beaverton and on Gretchen Schumacher's home in nearby Aloha, where Gretchen lived with her mother, Lila. Tina LaPlante stayed there, too, from time to time, and occupied an extra bedroom. In Wilson's home, they hoped to find Kathy's checkbook, wallet, remaining credit cards, driver's license, and other items of identification bearing her name, and, of course, her gold necklace and diamond pendant. Unfortunately, they didn't turn up any of those items there.

At Gretchen's residence, they seized a sheet of notebook paper from an upstairs bedroom that had been converted into a television room or den. The notebook paper had writing on it which referred to a car-rental business in Portland. In the bedroom that Tina had occupied they also found an address book that contained Michael Lissy's name and number. It appeared to be Tina's "little black book," they decided as they thumbed through it. Although helpful to their case, the address book and notebook paper were still just more circumstantial evidence.

Davis and Poppe went back to Tina for clarification on some of the details. They wanted to know about the rental car, which had by now come up at least twice in connection with Gretchen. Once when Starbuck told them about Gretchen and her alleged involvement, and again when they searched Gretchen's residence and found the sheet of notebook paper.

Now that Tina was essentially working for them and had little choice in the matter if she wanted to stay out of jail, Tina confirmed for Davis and Poppe that the plan had initially called for Gretchen and Wilson to rent a car in which they would drive to Eugene to carry out the murder. Wilson's driver's license had been suspended, which was the reason he needed Gretchen to drive him to Eugene, and they needed a rental car, in part because Tina doubted that her old car could make the trip. Because they were dealing with such a tight time frame, nobody really wanted to take the chance with Tina's car and the responsibility of renting one had been passed on to her. Most importantly, however, Tina, Wilson, and Gretchen didn't want to take the chance of being seen in a car that could ultimately be traced back to them.

But Tina had been unable to rent a car because they lacked a valid credit card, and none of them had enough money to put up a large cash deposit. As a result, Wilson and Gretchen had no choice but to drive to Eugene in Tina's 1973 Oldsmobile after all.

On Thursday, October 11, 1984, Davis and Poppe decided that it was time to move on Wilson. They met Tina LaPlante at 6 P.M. in a parking lot at Southeast Eighty-second Avenue and Stark Street. The two detectives accompanied Tina to a nearby telephone booth from where she called a number and asked to speak with Dave Wilson. Wilson wasn't there but was expected shortly, and a meeting was arranged at a nearby house, the home of one of Tina and Wilson's mutual friends, located in the 400 block of Southeast Seventy-fifth Avenue, for approximately thirty minutes later. When the phone call was concluded, they returned to the parking lot at Eight-second and Stark where they met with Sergeant Ralph Radmer and Officers Steve Bechard, Dave Jimerfield, and Wayne Baldassare, each assigned to vice/narcotics of the Portland Police Bureau's swing shift. There were several additional officers there to assist them, including a female officer who was responsible for taping the body-wire equipment onto Tina's body.

After the recording devices were attached to her body, Tina drove to the house where she had arranged to meet Wilson. Detectives Davis and Poppe, along with several of the officers, took up their positions one-half block south of the house. The recording equipment was rolling. Tina was obviously very nervous as evidenced by her heavy breathing. She nervously lit up a cigarette, tuned her car radio to a rock station, and waited for a few moments, to calm herself down a bit, before walking up to the house.

She hadn't seen Wilson for a few days, and she really didn't know how he would react to her. She hoped to God that he didn't pat her down or otherwise try to touch her. If he found out that she was helping the cops, he would most certainly try to kill her with his powerful hands, just as he had killed Kathy. But the cops kept her in near-constant sight, except for the short time that she would be inside the house. The plan, if it worked, called for her to get Wilson outside, into the yard, where they could watch them as they listened to their conversation.

Tina was scared, terrified really, as she approached the house. Her heart was beating hard, so hard that it seemed like it might leap out of her chest at any moment. But she had to remain cool, at least on the outside, and go through with it. It was her only ticket to freedom for getting mixed up in an insidiously evil plot that she should have never become involved with in the first place. She took a deep breath, then knocked on the door. A man she knew answered the door.

Wilson wasn't there yet, but was expected at any time, he told her. The man offered Tina a beer, which she accepted, and they made small talk for the next several minutes until they heard a car door slam shut outside.

"I wonder if that's Dave?" Tina asked as she sat her partially drank beer down on a table. She moved hurriedly toward the front door and opened it. She didn't want to give Wilson a chance to come inside. If he made it into the house, he might not want to go back outside. There was no question that she felt safer deceiving him outside where the cops could keep an eye on her.

"Well hello there," Wilson said with a grin when he saw who had opened the door.

"Hi," Tina said. "What's goin' on, huh?" She moved toward the outside. "I can only stay a minute, so let's go step outside and talk. Okay?"

"It's cold, man," Wilson said, complaining about the evening October chill as they stood outside the house. "You know, I'd expected to be arrested by now."

"Yeah," Tina agreed.

From their vantage point half a block up the

street, the cops could see Tina and Wilson near the front door of the house, but they could not distinguish many details, just two figures talking to each other in the dark. For that reason, they needed to confirm Wilson's identity visually, and Officer Jimerfield, wearing street clothes, drew the lucky straw to walk down the sidewalk in front of the house. Just before making the short jaunt, Jimerfield had looked at a Portland Police Bureau mug shot of Wilson, taken during a prior arrest unrelated to the Lissy case. When he returned to his colleagues after walking around the block, he told them that Tina was in fact talking to David Wilson.

"Do you know if anybody else has been subpoenaed, or anything?" Wilson asked.

"No," Tina said.

"Well, I think they're at a standstill," Wilson stated. "They might not have been able to get an indictment."

"Are you sure?" Tina asked.

"Well, I can't be sure," Wilson said. "I mean, I'm sure they would have arrested me by now."

"I don't know," Tina offered. "They probably wanted to get enough to make it stick."

"What else can they get?" Wilson asked. "The only thing they possibly could have gotten was hair an' prints."

"That's all they could have gotten from you in the room?" Tina was fishing, trying to get Wilson to say something—anything—incriminating that would place him at the crime scene.

"I don't think they could get any prints," Wilson stated confidently. "I don't think they could come up with any prints in the room. I know exactly what I touched."

"What?" Tina asked, pushing.

"I touched an ashtray," Wilson admitted. "Picked up an ashtray. But I took it and wiped it clean with the bedspread. And I left it settin', in fact I left it settin' right on the bed." Wilson seemed proud of himself, as if the ashtray with no fingerprints would taunt the police.

"Yeah," Tina said.

"And everything else I touched left the room with me," Wilson confessed.

"What all did you take out of the room? Seriously, 'cause I'm hearin' about these credit cards. And I asked you (on another occasion) what you did with them and you said they were stashed. Where are they?"

"They aren't stashed," Wilson said. He thought for a moment, then added: "Well, some of them are stashed. But . . . I won't tell nobody where they are."

"I'm not askin' you *where*," Tina said. "I'm just askin' if you've got 'em. I mean, you could go back and get 'em if you tried, right?"

"Um-huh," Wilson agreed. "Except that part of them I spread around in Eugene where somebody'd pick 'em up and possibly use 'em. And that's what happened. That's why they took the handwriting analysis. The checks, everything."

"You got checks?"

"Well, somebody used 'em."

"What all did you take out of Kathy's room? Everything, exactly. I don't even know. I've heard things about jewelry."

"Yeah," Wilson agreed, nodding his head affirmatively. "A necklace, credit cards, checks, her ID, everything."

"Could you get any of that stuff?" Tina asked. "Or is it gone?"

"Most of it's gone," Wilson said. "Because that same night, you see, I spread some around."

"You spread 'em around the same night of the murder?"

"Um-huh," Wilson said. "You understand why? So somebody'd use it."

"Right."

"They got so many goddamned directions, got so many leads in Eugene that this probably drove them up the fuckin' wall." Wilson seemed proud of himself again.

"Cool," Tina said. "You know, my lawyer came up to me and said something about her hair being pulled out and being strangled. What all did you do to her?"

"Let's sit in your car or somethin'," Wilson urged.

"No, let's just stand here."

"I'm fuckin' freezin'," Wilson argued. But he saw that Tina wasn't going to move. "I originally gagged her, then the gag didn't work."

"You gagged her mouth?" Tina asked.

"Yeah," Wilson agreed. "It wouldn't work,

and then I pulled the gag off and talked to her for a while."

"Tell me what she said," Tina demanded. "She knew Michael was settin' her up?"

"Yeah," Wilson said. "That's what she asked me. She says, 'Why did Michael set me up?' She didn't realize that I was gonna kill her."

"Yeah, go on."

"In fact, she got really comfortable with me," Wilson said. He seemed to enjoy reliving Kathy's murder, especially being able to relate the more intimate details to a female that he hoped to bed down with in the near future. It seemed to turn him on. "We just laid on the bed and talked for quite a while. Gretchen says (later, after the murder), 'You took so long . . . I almost left you.' "

"Oh really," Tina said. "She didn't go up in the room at all?"

"Gretchen never went nowhere near the motel," Wilson said. He then turned the conversation away from Gretchen: "I got the shit scared out of me. Do you know what? Last night I found, in my bed under my pillow, a book of matches. They said 'Valley River Inn.' "

"Oh fuck!" Tina exclaimed. "Was the room number on it?"

"Somebody put that there," Wilson stated.

"Oh, God."

"I never took no fucking matches," Wilson insisted.

"Did it have the room number on it?"

"No, it didn't say the room number," Wilson said.

"How did you get in?" Tina asked. "Michael said you could get in by saying you're 'Steve.' "

"I never had to say I was anybody," Wilson said. "I knocked on the door and she invited me in. Took my jacket, hung it up."

"What happened when you guys were laying on the bed?" Tina asked.

"She started asking questions," Wilson said, laughing. "And I said, 'I ain't tellin' you nothin', so she said, 'How come Michael set me up?' I said, 'Michael who?' And I said, 'Are you married? You're married.' And she said, 'Yeah, to Michael.' "

"Michael Lissy," Tina said.

"I said, 'Michael who?' " Wilson stated. "I says, 'Michael. I don't know any Michael.' And anyway, she started askin' me a lot of questions . . . like, 'What are you doin' this for?' and 'What does he want?' I says, 'I ain't answerin' no questions. You want to talk business, we'll talk business.' I just told her, 'Get on your stomach.' " Wilson was really enjoying this.

"And then what?" Tina asked.

"And then, the gag was pulled down around her throat, right? I told her to roll on her stomach. Then I crawled on top of her and just reached down and grabbed the gag, and I just, I twisted it."

"How long 'til she died?" Tina asked.

"She never moved a muscle," Wilson said.

"She just laid there and it was just . . . she was out instantly . . . it takes two seconds to put somebody out when you cut off the, uh, jugular vein . . . without ever choking her, I cut off her breath. . . ."

"Don't you do that to me," Tina said, thinking ahead to the deal she'd made with him about going to bed with him before he turned himself in. "Shit!"

"I was just sayin'," Wilson offered, "that I could make you go out without killin' ya, just make you go out . . . two to three seconds you'd be out like a light . . . but . . . she was still breathin'."

"Oh."

"So I said, 'Die bitch!' " Wilson said.

"Did she hear you?" Tina asked.

"No, she was out."

"God."

"And then I just twisted (the gag) without lettin' go," Wilson said. "I just got up and I walked around her once and twisted it tighter and then I held it there. Do you want to hear everything?"

"Yeah, go ahead."

" 'Til her eyes bulged out."

"Her eyes bulged out?" Tina asked.

" 'Til, 'til her face turned purple."

"Oooh," Tina said, feeling sick inside.

"And her body quit twitchin'."

"At least she wasn't awake for it all," Tina said, a hopeful tone in her voice.

"No," Wilson said. "She was out cold. She never felt nothin'."

"God, doesn't that freak you out?" Tina asked.

Wilson didn't answer the question. Instead he said: "What I did is wipe my prints off the ashtray, went over and went through her purse. I just reached in and took things out . . . took a briefcase full of shit."

"What happened to that briefcase the night you took it out of my car?" Tina asked. "Remember I said to get rid of it?"

"I did. I threw it in the trash."

"Over there?" Tina gestured toward the garbage can nearby.

"Yeah," Wilson said. "And then somebody I know picked it up."

"God."

"So I got it back again. Do you know that briefcase was here?"

"Are you serious?" Tina asked.

"It's gone now," Wilson said.

"Good. Man. . . ."

Wilson had talked about "doing business" with Kathy the night he killed her, and that had interested Tina enough to bring him back to that topic.

"You mean if she were to have offered you more than five thousand dollars like Michael paid you, you wouldn't have done it (killed her)?" Tina asked.

"No," Wilson answered. "I'd have taken her money and then did it."

"Oh, shit. Goddamn," Tina said, suddenly more aware just how cold-blooded and calculating Wilson really was. And here she was, talking to him, listening to him get sexually aroused as he related details of Kathy's murder to her.

"Have you ever murdered anybody before, besides Kathy?" Tina asked.

"Yup."

"So it wasn't so hard to kill her, huh?"

"It's nothin'," Wilson said. "There's one thing you gotta see . . . I can adjust to any situation. You know I can ignore it like it isn't there . . . if the money is right."

"If Michael pulls some shit, are you gonna go right up and say, 'Hey, I killed Kathy for Michael for five thousand bucks'? Will you tell them that?"

"After the fact, I'm saying after I'm convicted. What's more, after I'm convicted, if I rolled over on him they'll probably release me from prison."

"That's true," Tina said. "They probably would. Have you got anything else you want to tell me?"

"Not that I can think of."

"I'm glad you told me what you did in the room because, man, I was thinkin', man, you beat her and you did bad things to her."

"No, her hair got caught in the gag and twisted," Wilson said. "Got all entangled."

"Was that after she was already dead?"

"When I tied the gag, her hair got caught in it," Wilson said. "So when I grabbed it and I twisted it, and then I twisted it again, then when I took it off her, I just pulled the hair out. All this hair was all over."

"We're gonna have to get it where you talk to Michael and scare the shit out of him," Tina said, " 'cause I think he fuckin' might run off. You let him know that you can prove his involvement."

"I can prove it," Wilson said. "I got evidence that I can have planted on him, near him . . . and if I do it, I'll have it put someplace where . . . I'll flat fuckin' come back at him why he told me he'd give me two hundred thousand dollars if I went ahead and took the fall. He didn't pay me the money, so that's why I'm speakin' up now . . . you get the idea . . . and you better believe the fuckin' jury will eat that up. They'd look at him and think, 'Well, that lowlife' . . . yes, I gotta talk to him. The sooner the better."

"Okay, tell me exactly what I should tell him next time I talk to him," Tina demanded.

"Tell him I have to have more information, because I have to have the story straight," Wilson said. "I can't go in half-cocked because they're gonna browbush me and they're gonna put so much pressure on me that it's gonna be unreal. And I gotta be able to look 'em dead in the eye and say, 'Yeah, this is the way it is.' And they're gonna ask me another time and I'm gonna say it again." Wilson seemed to know the routine of police grilling.

"You think any of your hair got in there, in her hotel room?" Tina asked.

"Hair falls out all the time . . . I shouldn't have listened to the part about . . . him wanting it to look like a rape . . . or whatever his scheme was . . . 'cause, when it came down to it, I couldn't rape her. In fact she had to help me *get off.*"

"Did you get off?"

"Yeah, but I never did fuck her," Wilson said. "There was *no violence* in the world whatsoever. I hit her in the stomach once to get her attention. But it wasn't hard enough to hurt. It scared the fuck out of her. And then I just pulled back like I was gonna hit her."

Wilson demonstrated to Tina how he had drawn his fist back, and from down the street the detectives suddenly became alarmed. They thought, even if only for an instant, that Wilson was going to strike Tina. She apparently thought so, too.

"Don't fuckin' do that to me, man," Tina said.

"You know I'd never hit you," Wilson said.

"Fuck."

"Unless we don't get together." Wilson was talking about part of the deal where Tina was supposed to go to bed with him prior to him going to jail for Lissy. He began to stroke her arms.

"I know our deal, okay?" she said, moving away from him.

"Well, tomorrow night?"

"I don't know if I can," Tina said. "I can give you a call tomorrow . . . at six."

"You will give me a call."

"Yeah, you don't have to stick around here."

"Okay, like you did last time?"

"Well, I did you know," Tina said as she climbed into her car.

"Okay," Wilson said.

Tina started the engine and turned on the radio. It would be the last time Wilson saw her before going to court. Tina, trembling inside and out, drove straight back to the parking lot at Eighty-second and Stark.

"You ought to be in Hollywood," said one of the cops, a big grin on his face.

Twenty

At 8:33 the next evening, Friday, October 12, 1984, Tina LaPlante was again escorted to the Portland Police Bureau in the downtown Justice Center Building by Detectives Lloyd Davis and David Poppe. She was there to call Michael Lissy again, to try and get him to say something else that would incriminate himself in his wife's death so that the police could capture it on tape. Nobody answered the phone at Lissy's parents' home on the Oregon coast on the first attempt. But on the second attempt a few minutes later, Lissy answered.

"Hello," Lissy said.

"Michael?" Tina asked.

"Yeah."

"Hi, this is Tina. How you doin'?"

"Okay."

"Can you go to a phone booth?" she asked.

"Yeah," Lissy replied. "Why? Is it important?"

"Yeah." Tina gave him the number.

"Remember the code?" Tina asked. She was

really setting him up for the cops this time. She was good, especially at deception.

"Yeah," Lissy said. "I'll call you in about five minutes."

A few minutes later the phone rang, and Tina picked it up on the first ring. They all agreed that it should appear as if she were standing in front of a bank of pay telephones waiting for an incoming call, and picking it up on the first ring bolstered that effect.

"Hi. Guess what?" Tina asked.

"What?"

"I just called Dave's house."

"Yeah," Lissy said, waiting for more.

"His mom said they took him away tonight for murder," Tina said. "They don't know what kind of murder. They just took him away." Wilson hadn't yet been arrested, but his arrest was imminent, and would be behind bars before Lissy had a chance to do any investigating on his own.

"Huh." Lissy was stunned.

"I talked to him last night," Tina said, "and you know, told him what you told me."

"Yeah." Lissy seemed deep in thought.

"He seems real worried about the money."

"Yeah."

"And I was assuring him," Tina said, "that you wouldn't take off . . . he thought you might take the insurance money and split."

"Oh, no," Lissy said.

"And he was telling me if you did, he'd prove that you'd hired him," Tina said.

"Yeah, I know," Lissy said. "There's no problem. Where you calling from?"

"Pay phone at Meier and Frank's," Tina lied. "It's closin' pretty soon. This is a good place for me to talk 'cause it's downstairs."

"Okay." Lissy apparently bought it. "They did pick him up tonight?"

"Yep," Tina replied. "I'm not sure what time."

"Ummmm." Lissy either had doubts about what he was being told, or he was deep in thought, perhaps planning what his next move would be.

"Oh, and he only got half the story," Tina said. "He still needs to know a lot more."

"Well, I don't know what else to say 'cause there's no way to talk to him," Lissy said. "Which Meier and Frank are you at? Downtown?" He couldn't seem to get his mind off the location from which Tina was calling. He was definitely suspicious.

"Uh-huh," Tina said.

"Oh. They're open 'til nine?"

"Yep."

"Oh. I didn't think the downtown one stayed open that late."

"Yep." Tina didn't want to talk about it. She was afraid he might be able to detect something in her voice that would reveal the setup.

"Okay. What's that noise?" Lissy asked.

"I don't know."

"Well, listen," he insisted.

"I'm sure it's nothin'," Tina said. "I'm at a pay phone. Don't freak out on me."

"Okay," Lissy said. "Chances are then that they'll be picking us up, too."

"Why do you think that?"

"Well," he said, "they probably won't pick one up without pickin' everybody up. But do you think he'll hold with the story?"

"I didn't pay him what he wanted."

"Was he upset about that?" Lissy asked.

"Umm, yeah. I mean yesterday, last night when I talked to him . . . he wanted real badly for me to get together with him."

"Well, we'll just have to see what happens," Lissy said. "Let's hope he holds tight."

"He said if you didn't pay, if you don't pay him, he can plant stuff," Tina said. "He said he could plant credit cards."

"I believe that can happen," Lissy said. "Okay, uh, well thanks for the warning."

"Yeah, okay," Tina said. "So how's your sex life been?"

"Terrible," he said. "You want to come down and date me?"

"No," Tina replied. "I don't need the money, really."

"Is that right?"

"Well, I do. But I mean, how am I gonna have somebody watch my kid and come clear down there?"

"Well, bring him with you," Lissy suggested.

"He doesn't like to watch those kinds of things."

"I don't have a sex life down here," Lissy said.

"I bet," Tina said. "So what do you do?"

"Jack off. That's about it," Lissy said. "I'm serious. Okay, no matter what they hit you with, you don't know nothin'. Anything major breaks, give me a call. Hang tough, don't be surprised if you get arrested."

"Don't tell me that," Tina said.

"Well, I just think that if they've issued it (arrest warrant) against him, they've done it against everybody," Lissy said. "But they'd want to pick him up first. And then probably you, and then probably me. Bye."

"Huh?"

"Goodbye. And good luck."

Early the next morning, Detectives Lloyd Davis and David Poppe began coordinating efforts to arrest Michael Lissy and David Wilson. Shortly before 9 A.M. Davis and Poppe had everyone in place, standing by at Lissy's parents' home at Lincoln Beach, near Depoe Bay, on the Oregon coast and at David Wilson's residence in Beaverton. When the go-ahead signal was given, Davis and Poppe, along with several uniformed officers, converged on the Lissy home while Washington County authorities did likewise at the Wilson residence one hundred miles away. Neither man seemed particularly surprised by their arrest, and they remained quiet during their respective two-hour drive to the Lane County Jail in Eugene.

Upon their arrival, Lissy and Wilson were booked separately so that they wouldn't have any opportunity to make contact with one another. They were held without bail on accusations of aggravated murder. Each was also charged with murder, robbery, rape, and sexual abuse, all in the first degree, in connection with Kathryn Ann Martini-Lissy's death.

"The state is alleging that this was a contract killing, a killing for hire . . . that Lissy contracted for pay with Wilson for the death of Lissy's wife," said J. Pat Horton, then the Lane County District Attorney, to reporters at a news conference that afternoon.

Lissy's parents were devastated, as was Wilson's mother, by the events that had transpired during a few short hours that day and had resulted in their sons' being arrested for murder, a contract killing at that.

"The only thing we know is that he is innocent of any wrongdoing in this," Lissy's mother, Patricia, told reporters. "The Sunday before she was murdered, they were here and she told me they decided to start their family. They were so happy. She was a wonderful, wonderful girl. And he loved her very much. We all did."

Several days later Lissy and Wilson were indicted on identical charges by a Lane County grand jury. Both men pleaded innocent, and were continued held without bail. Now that Lissy and Wilson were in custody, everyone in the law enforcement community was committed to making sure that they remained in police custody.

In reviewing the facts of the case, Lane County District Attorney J. Pat Horton knew that it was going to be a tough one, despite the top-notch detective work that Davis and Poppe had accomplished. That's why he assigned it to one of his top deputies, Brian Barnes, for prosecution. If anyone could convince a jury of Lissy's guilt, Barnes could.

In putting the case together Barnes noted that Lissy, when first informed of Kathy's death, had intimated that Kathy was a drug user and suggested that her death was related to such illegal activities. He had also suggested that Kathy had been involved in romantic encounters while in Eugene on business, and hinted that one of the men he said she had dated might be responsible for the killing. Lissy had indicated that he was not aware of any insurance on his wife's life.

Based on the facts, Barnes had no difficulty seeing through Lissy's feigned innocence. He saw that Lissy had regular encounters with prostitutes, and that during these encounters he had solicited help in finding a hit man to get rid of his wife for him. His motive was clearly two-fold: First, he wanted to obtain the nearly $200,000 in life insurance if Kathy died while traveling on company business; secondly, he wanted to get back together with his previous wife, Elise Dunn. To accomplish those goals, Lissy believed he had to kill Kathy, and he very much wanted to kill Brad Lemmer, Elise's new boyfriend. Elise would testify to those claims, as would others.

Barnes noted that the investigation showed that Paul McNeil had met with Lissy at least three times concerning one of Lissy's plots to kill Kathy. In fact, during one of the detectives' follow-up calls, McNeil had told Davis and Poppe that Lissy had wanted Kathy dead so that he could collect on the insurance. Lissy had wanted to know about lethal drugs which could be mixed with cocaine and alcohol, which he had hoped he would ultimately be able to use to cause Kathy's death. Lissy figured that McNeil, a certified nursing assistant, would know about such things. But according to McNeil, Lissy had also suggested a car "accident" in Eugene as another means to do her in. Just as he had told others, Lissy had told McNeil that Kathy's life insurance would be more if she was out of town on business when she died.

And on and on it went. Elise Dunn, Paul McNeil, Bary Franklin, Beth Cumley, Monica Glenn, Molly Griggs, and Tina LaPlante, among others, would testify to Lissy's plans and schemes in a trial that would be dubbed in the national media, "Oregon's Most Fantastic Contract Killing Ever."

* * *

On Wednesday, November 14, 1984, Gretchen Schumacher was arrested at her home in Aloha, Oregon, when Davis and Poppe learned that she had returned. She was picked up on allegations that she drove David Wilson to Eugene on the night of the murder for a mere $250, and was subsequently charged with aggravated murder in connection with Kathy's death.

"She was charged as a principal," said the district attorney, "namely one that aided and abetted in the murder." Like Wilson and Lissy had done, Schumacher pleaded innocent to the charges.

Two days later, on Friday, November 16, Wendy Whiteman was driving north on Interstate 5, heading toward Portland when her car, without warning, had a mechanical breakdown. She was about a mile south of the Corvallis exit when she pulled her car onto the freeway shoulder and brought it to a stop. She was approximately fifty miles north of Eugene.

Wendy climbed out of her car and began walking along the freeway, hoping to find a telephone booth from which she could call for help, when she suddenly saw something shiny out of the corner of her eye. When she looked at it directly, she saw that it was a brass makeup case and a cassette tape lying on the gravel alongside the freeway. She picked up the items, and saw the name Kathryn Ann Martini engraved onto the case. Because the name sounded familiar, she placed the items inside her own purse and took them with her.

The next day, after she realized that the items were related to the ongoing murder case, Wendy took the items to the Eugene Police Department where they were seized as evidence. An officer drove Wendy back to the location where she had found the makeup case and cassette tape. After searching for a few minutes, the officer found a small card, similar in size to a credit card. But it had small holes punched into it, and it appeared to be some type of computer card, possibly a bank or identification card. More importantly, however, the card bore Kathy's name on it.

Twenty-one

Things clearly weren't working out the way that Michael Lissy had planned. David Wilson had not pleaded guilty or claimed responsibility for murdering Lissy's wife as Lissy had hoped he would. In fact, Wilson pleaded innocent to all of the charges. As one day followed another and eventually turned into weeks, it became increasingly apparent that Wilson wasn't going to take the fall for Lissy after all. To make matters worse for Lissy, he didn't know if Wilson and Schumacher had talked to the detectives or had worked out a deal with the prosecutor's office. And it came as quite a shock to Lissy when he learned that he was going to be tried *first* for his wife's murder.

Pretrial motions by Lissy's team of defense attorneys, Ronald R. Sticka and John Halpern, were heard before Lane County Circuit Court Judge William A. Beckett. Sticka and Halpern were contending that several items seized from Gretchen's house were beyond the scope of the search warrant used to confiscate the items. Judge Beckett apparently agreed, and struck a blow to the prosecution's case by not allowing such items as Tina LaPlante's "little black book" and the piece of notebook paper with the rental car information.

Sticka and Halpern also filed motions to suppress other evidence. They wanted to keep such items as those confiscated from Lissy and Kathy's condominium from being admitted as state's exhibits, contending that the search warrants used to seize the evidence had been obtained illegally. They claimed the methods used by police to obtain a "positive identification" placing Lissy at the Valley River Inn the night Kathy was murdered were faulty. Their argument was that Bonita J. Golliher, the night maintenance supervisor at the hotel, was shown only Lissy's photograph, not several of individuals including Lissy with similar features and build-up.

Sticka argued that the search warrant evidence was based on "the suggestive photo identification process." Sticka said: "There is no other evidence, to my knowledge, to suggest that the defendant was in Eugene the night of the murder." Sticka also sought to suppress the electronic surveillance tapes of conversations between Lissy and Molly Griggs, Lissy and Tina LaPlante, and Tina LaPlante and David Wilson, contending that they violated Lissy's state and federal constitutional rights.

Bonita Golliher testified during the pretrial

motions that she saw a large man with a beard and hair similar to Lissy's during her shift on the night of July 5.

"I never have been positive," testified Golliher. "I've always said this looks like the man who walked through the lobby. He caught my eye because he was an unusually big person that looked neat. I never made a statement that said I was positive."

Detective Lloyd Davis countered by testifying that he believed, at the time he wrote the affidavit in support of the search warrant for Lissy's home, van, and business, that Golliher had positively identified Lissy as the man she had seen in the hotel lobby. Judge Beckett said he would study the motions and consider the prosecution's arguments before making a decision.

Meanwhile, in an attempt to convince Beckett that there was enough evidence to show that a conspiracy existed and that a jury should be allowed to hear all of the wiretap conversations, Deputy District Attorney Brian Barnes placed Tina LaPlante on the stand and she was duly sworn.

"Miss LaPlante, how old are you?" Barnes asked.

"Twenty," Tina answered.

"Do you know the defendant, Michael Lissy?"

"Yes, I do."

"For approximately how many years or months have you known him?"

"I think well over a year. A year and a few months."

"Where did you meet him?" Barnes asked.

"Portland," Tina replied.

"Did you work for him?"

"Yes. I worked in his scuba shop."

"Did you have certain types of social engagements with him?"

"Like what do you mean?"

"Did you have what you referred to as 'dates' with him?"

"Yes," Tina said. "When I worked, I worked like three hours a day in the store. Then I dated him a few times a week."

"Did he pay you for these dates?"

"Yes."

"Going back to June of last year, did Mr. Lissy ask you or have conversations with you about having a person killed?"

"Objection," Sticka interrupted. "Leading nature of the questions."

"Sustained," Beckett ruled.

"Did you have conversations with Mr. Lissy about a woman in Eugene?" Barnes asked.

"Uh, about a woman," Tina repeated.

"Where was that conversation?"

"Across the street from the scuba-diving shop in his old apartment, or Elise's old apartment."

"Was that during the course of a date with him?"

"Yes," Tina testified. Over Sticka's objection to hearsay, Tina was allowed to explain that a friend of hers had told her that Lissy had wanted to date her for sexual services. It was during a date at the apartment on Barbur Boulevard, across from the scuba shop, that he had asked her to find a hit man for him.

"I dated him," she said, "then he asked me if I knew somebody—somebody that would kill somebody. First he asked me . . . if I could do it . . . like hit a lady over the head or something . . . but he seen that I was pregnant and . . . you know, I told him I couldn't do it. So he asked if I could get somebody for him."

"What did he tell you he wanted done?" Barnes asked.

"He said he wanted a lady strang—preferably strangled and raped, or like hit over the head or something."

"Did he indicate how much he'd be willing to pay for that?"

"Yeah. He said five thousand dollars."

"What did you tell him?"

"I told him I'd get a hold of him in a few days . . . just told him I'd check into it."

"Did the defendant indicate to you where the person would be . . . whether the person that he wanted killed would be in Portland or elsewhere?"

"I think later, when he said it was out of town."

"How much later?"

"A week, maybe."

"At the time he was originally talking to you

about wanting to hire someone to kill a lady, what did you think of that? Did you think he was serious?"

"Oh, yeah," Tina said without hesitation. "Yeah, I thought he was serious."

"Did you look for someone for him?"

Tina explained how she had found David Wilson at the home of Linda Crewes, the Tweak House.

"We were doing drugs in the bedroom," Tina said. "There was about four people in there, and I was just talking, you know, and I go, 'Does anybody know anybody who would kill somebody . . . for a certain amount of money?' And this guy . . . Dave Wilson, said he will, 'I'll do it,' something to that effect . . . we did our drugs, and later he pulled me aside and said he would do it."

"Dave Wilson did?"

"Yes."

"Do you recall what he specifically said?"

"He just said he—something like he's done that kind of thing before," Tina testified. "And that he'd do it, or whatever."

"What did you tell him?"

"Well, I told him he'd get five thousand dollars, and the money would be delivered afterwards, after it was done."

"How did you know that?"

"Well, 'cause Michael told me that I'd pick it up every week for however many weeks makes five thousand dollars."

"He told you this before you met and talked with Mr. Wilson?"

"Yes."

"Did you relay Wilson's statements back to the defendant about him being willing to do it?"

"Yes . . . I called him and told him . . ."

"You'd become aware, didn't you, when Kathryn Lissy was killed in Eugene, at least from the news media?"

"Yes, I found out that it was his wife."

"The first time that Wilson said, 'I'll do it,'— about how long was that before the killing?"

"A few days," Tina replied. "I don't think it was more than four days."

In response to Barnes's questions, Tina explained how she went back and told Lissy that she had a hit man for him. She had voiced her concern about Wilson being a "druggy," and had questioned his reliability. But Lissy, she said, was adamant that he wanted Wilson for the job. He had said that it couldn't wait, that the killing had to occur by Thursday, July 5. Lissy wanted to talk to Wilson as soon as possible.

Tina said she picked up Wilson, called Lissy on his beeper, and arranged to meet Lissy. Lissy and Wilson talked for a short time in Lissy's car, and the next day Tina drove Wilson to Lissy's store in the Hollywood area of Portland.

"Did you hear the conversation between them?" Barnes asked.

"A little bit, I heard it," she said.

"What did that involve?"

"I think Michael just asked him if he would do it," Tina said. "He said he wanted her strangled and raped, if possible . . . he said he'd give me the information about where it was (to occur) . . . a couple of days later."

Tina explained that Lissy had told her that the woman he wanted killed would be out of town. He had not mentioned to her, however, prior to Kathy's death, that the woman he had wanted killed was his wife.

"Had he told you, prior to her death, anything about insurance?" Barnes asked.

"I really can't remember," Tina replied. "Right afterwards I knew for sure, because he was saying he couldn't get the insurance money if they thought that he killed his wife, or whatever."

"After her death he told you that?"

"Yeah, for sure afterwards . . ."

"Did he indicate to you how much insurance was involved?"

"I think he changed it—different amounts. I can't remember."

Following the murder, Tina said, she transferred money from Lissy to Wilson on several occasions. The first transfer occurred the day after the murder. Tina had gone to Lissy's old apartment on Barbur Boulevard to pick up the money. Following Lissy's instructions, Tina had found $1,000, taped underneath a toilet seat.

"Was that an arrangement you made with Mr. Lissy?" Barnes asked.

"Yes," Tina replied. "I was supposed to go

once a week and clean the place a little bit, and get the money from under the toilet seat."

"He'd hide the money there, you'd pick it up, then do what with it?"

"Then I would take it to Dave."

"Did you deliver money to Wilson on many occasions?"

"Yes, up 'til he got five thousand dollars."

"Did the process of picking up and delivering the money change?"

"Yes, after the—second time. I think I picked it up there one more time, and then Michael said, 'I don't want to do that anymore,' because the police are getting hot on his tail or whatever. So he met me places . . . like at the Fred Meyer's on Barbur Boulevard to deliver it, and Beaverton Fred Meyer's . . . and up by the zoo."

"What did you do with the money he was giving you on those occasions?"

"Well, at one time Dave Wilson was in jail (on a charge unrelated to Kathy's murder), so I just buried it in my backyard."

"Was all the money that Lissy gave you on those occasions for the purpose of paying Wilson the five thousand dollars?"

"Yes, besides what I got here and there."

Tina also testified about the scheme Lissy devised in which Wilson would take the fall for him for $25,000. Lissy, she said, had been worrying that he wouldn't get the insurance money if he was convicted of Kathy's murder, and he didn't want to go to jail, either. Worrying that he would eventually be arrested and charged with Kathy's murder after the hair samples taken from him during the grand-jury proceedings were compared to samples obtained as evidence from Kathy's hotel room, Wilson agreed to do it for Lissy. Wilson had felt that he could get off easier, perhaps on a manslaughter charge, if he confessed to Kathy's death by saying that he had killed her in anger during the course of a drug deal.

"Did you see Mr. Lissy give Mr. Wilson any money prior to the murder?" Barnes asked.

"Yeah," Tina replied. "He gave him a few hundred dollars when I took him to the scuba-diving shop to meet Michael. He gave him a few hundred dollars to rent a car, get a nice outfit and a haircut."

"Why did he feel a nice outfit and a haircut (were) needed?"

"So he could look respectable . . . Michael says he needs to look respectable to fit in with the place where the murder was going to happen."

"Did you eventually try to rent a car?"

"Yes, I think I ran around that day trying to rent one . . . but he didn't have the right ID, no credit cards, and stuff. . . ."

"Was he along, and anybody else along when you tried to rent the car?"

"Well, just Dave Wilson and my cousin Gretchen."

"Gretchen Schumacher?"

"Yes."

"Just prior to the murder, were you furnished information about where the place was that she was going to be?"

"Yes . . . I beeped Michael on his beeper . . . told him Dave was getting his hair cut, and he's got an outfit and everything. So Michael met me downtown . . . gave me a little matchbook—pretty sure it was a matchbook, or a little piece of paper—that said, Valley River Inn, Eugene. It had a room number . . . Dave Wilson was supposed to introduce himself as 'Steve' to get into the lady's room . . . and that she'd be expecting him."

"Did you relay the information, or did you give the information about the room number at the Valley River Inn to anyone?"

"Yes, I gave the whole thing to Dave. Told him everything, what to do."

"And eventually were you able to rent a car? Or whose car was used?"

"I couldn't rent a car," Tina responded. "It was like six o'clock, and it was time for him to go, so I just let him take my car, and my cousin drove him."

"That was Gretchen?"

"Yes."

"When did you next see Wilson?"

Tina explained that she saw Wilson later that same night, when Gretchen brought him back to Portland. Wilson told her that Kathy let him into her room when he got there, and had asked Wilson why Michael was setting her up.

"Did he indicate to you what he'd done to her?"

"He said he was trying to rape her, but he couldn't—I don't know if he—he just couldn't do it, and he said that she . . . was *helping him,* like maybe she just thought she was going to get raped or something. But he just said that she was helping him . . . and he said something about rolling over and then he said he choked her . . . he showed me his fingers, and they were all swollen and red."

"Did you have any conversation with Mr. Lissy about Wilson doing things in Eugene, apart from killing the woman?"

"Michael gave me some money to get the heat off him," Tina said. "He wanted Dave to go down and push himself on somebody and beat somebody else, so that it would look like the same thing. You know, like somebody around Eugene did it . . . if Dave came down here and attacked another lady and beat her and tried to strangle her, then it would look like some freak from around here was doing it."

"Did you talk to Dave Wilson about him doing it?"

"Yes."

"Was any money ever given to Dave Wilson?"

"For that reason?"

"For that purpose."

"Yes."

"And where did that money come from?"

"Came from Michael."

"Did you ever talk with Dave Wilson about (Becky Norton)?"

"I know he was pushing himself on her and trying to make her say that this guy was raping her."

"What I was asking, if Dave Wilson ever indicated he'd approached (Becky Norton) as a part of this deal, to go down to Eugene?"

"Yes."

"Prior to the tapes, did you have any discussion with David Wilson about him planting other evidence . . . in Eugene? I'm particularly referring to some credit cards."

"I heard . . . from Dave . . . something about him passing some around Eugene. . . ."

Judge Beckett, after hearing Tina's testimony and after listening to the various wiretap recordings, ruled that Tina's testimony and the tape recordings could be presented to a jury. Beckett decided that the recordings were sufficient proof that a conspiracy existed between Lissy, David Wilson, Tina LaPlante, Gretchen Schumacher, and others to kill Kathryn Ann Martini-Lissy so that Lissy could collect on her life insurance.

Similarly, Beckett also ruled that most of the evidence seized by police at Lissy and Kathy's condominium would be admitted. The evidence in question had been the gun found inside

Lissy's van, and Kathy's insurance documents and will naming Lissy as the beneficiary.

Even as jury selection got underway on Thursday, January 17, 1985, the curious spectators crowded into Lane County Circuit Judge William Beckett's courtroom, leaving standing room only. It was a trial that Lane County's trial-goers didn't want to miss. Members of Lissy's family were present, as were Kathy's parents and other relatives.

By that afternoon, two of twelve prospective jurors had been dismissed because they had already formed an opinion as to Lissy's guilt. A third prospective juror was dismissed following a challenge by the defense and prosecuting attorneys. As Sticka questioned the prospective jurors, he asked them how they would be able to handle "hearing things you'd rather not hear." He also asked them their feelings about a "married man using prostitutes." Despite the potential difficulty, a jury of nine men and three women was seated by the next afternoon. The trial, which was expected to last two-and-a-half weeks, was set to begin.

Twenty-two

A steady stream of spectators filed into Courtroom Number Three, Lane County Circuit
Judge William Beckett's courtroom, on Monday,
January 21, 1985, the first day of Michael David
Lissy's trial before a jury. The constant drone
of the spectators halted suddenly when Lissy was
brought into the courtroom via the side door
used exclusively for prisoners. Lissy was neatly
groomed for the occasion. His hair had been
cut, and his beard neatly trimmed. Sporting a
suit and tie, Lissy didn't look like the despicable
character who was being portrayed as having
regularly cheated on his wife by cavorting with
prostitutes and drug addicts. He certainly didn't
look like the death plotter and fraud that the
prosecution was alleging him to be. In fact, if
appearances were all that was to be taken into
account, Lissy could have easily passed for one
of the lawyers representing him, or even the
prosecutor. He appeared calm as he confidently
took his seat at the defense table, as if he
thought he could easily beat the charges against
him.

Following a number of legal formalities, Deputy District Attorney Brian Barnes addressed the jury with his opening statements. In a very sharp and pointed tone, Barnes described the case in detail for the jury of nine men and three women. He painted a very graphic picture for them, a sort of "road map" that they could follow as they listened to the testimony of the witnesses. He cautioned them that Lissy was a skilled liar and a braggart, and that they should carefully weigh what they heard from him against what they heard from the other witnesses.

"When the police talked to him throughout the investigation, the defendant was lying through his teeth," Barnes stated. "The defendant, at that time, knew very well who had killed his wife because it was he who had instigated and solicited David Wilson to kill his wife . . . evidence will show that Lissy was a guy who continually engaged others to do the dirty work, no matter what level of crime it was . . . he worked his way up the ladder of serious crimes to this latest one, the biggest fraud of all. . . .

"And why?" Barnes continued. "Well, the evidence is going to show from these various witnesses who will be called . . . that he is a particularly degenerate individual who put money at the top of his list. The reason for this killing was pure and simple greed because Kathryn Martini-Lissy had insurance through her work that would pay approximately one hundred ninety thousand dollars if she happened to die while traveling on business, which, of course, she was doing while in Eugene."

Barnes explained that the jurors would hear tape recordings of conversations between Lissy and a police informant, Tina LaPlante, one of Lissy's "unindicted coconspirators" and former prostitute. Those recordings, said Barnes, would help prove that Lissy hired David Wilson to kill his wife. Barnes also told the jury that he would present testimony from Lissy's former wife, Elise Dunn, who would testify that Lissy told her he planned to kill Kathryn while she was in Boston on business so that he could collect her life insurance and reunite with her.

"He was very insistent that he wanted to reunite with Elise," said Barnes. Barnes also said that he would demonstrate the type of lying and deceit that Lissy had engaged in during the investigation, and later.

"It is a type of lying and deceit and trying to throw the police off the trail that will continue on through the whole investigation until he is arrested, and later it will continue on through this trial," Barnes said.

"Here is a guy that we will expect will try to convince you that he's not guilty of these charges that we are here having this trial on," Barnes continued. "The evidence that I outlined—and it is just an outline—will show a lot of things about the defendant and about other people. But what it is going to show you, beyond any reasonable doubt, is that the defendant unlawfully and intentionally solicited David Wilson to kill his wife. That, under Oregon law, ladies and gentlemen, is aggravated murder. That's what the state has to prove beyond a reasonable doubt. That is what we will prove beyond a reasonable doubt, no matter what Mr. Lissy says.

"Bear in mind as you hear the defense case, defense opening statement, the words of the defendant repeated over and over again, 'Just hang in there. There is always a chance you can beat it in court.' That is what this trial is about."

Ronald R. Sticka, one of Lissy's defense attorneys, presented a sharply contrasting argument in his opening statements: "May it please the court, counsel, ladies and gentlemen of the jury. You heard one side, that is the state's side of what they expect the evidence will show. I will make a few additional comments, attempting to frame the issues.

"There is one statement I wanted to address up front," Sticka continued. "Mr. Barnes, just before he finished, indicated something to the effect Mr. Lissy will try to convince you he is not guilty and that is what this trial is all about. That is an inaccurate statement, ladies and gentlemen. The burden is always on the state to prove guilt beyond a reasonable doubt. Mr. Lissy does not have any obligation to prove anything to you, one way or the other.

"Now, in fact, Mr. Lissy is going to testify in these proceedings, and the defense will submit evidence, and we are going to suggest a substantially different interpretation of the facts. Mr. Barnes has painted Mr. Lissy to be some sort of monster. We submit the evidence is going to show Mr. Lissy is not a monster. He is a man caught up in circumstances. Perhaps he's guilty of many things, but he is not guilty of murder."

Sticka portrayed Lissy as a liar and a braggart who tried to impress the pimps and prostitutes he regularly employed by making murder plans involving his wife.

"It was a situation that sadly backfired," Sticka contended. "Mr. Lissy was playing a sort of game with them, getting them wrapped up in something sinister and exciting and sort of morbid."

The reason Lissy was untruthful with the police during the investigation of Kathryn's murder, Sticka said, was because he was afraid and confused, and that he didn't know for certain who had actually killed his wife but that he was nonetheless especially afraid of Wilson. It was all a game of bragging and fantasizing that had gotten out of hand.

"Mr. Lissy was confronted with the fact (of a murder) already accomplished . . . by street people . . . a murder he did not intend," Sticka contended. Sticka insisted that Lissy loved his wife and had "every incentive" to keep her alive because of her career potential. Sticka portrayed Lissy as a man so depressed and distraught over his wife's death that he tried to commit suicide.

Sticka told the jurors that Kathryn had been in contact with some of the same street people that Lissy knew, including Gretchen Schumacher, because she had purchased cocaine and other drugs from those contacts. It seemed that Sticka was going to try and convince the jury that Kathryn was dead as a result, either directly or indirectly, of her own lifestyle, and not because of her husband's plotting.

Twenty-three

As the trial continued, a procession of witnesses took the stand, each relating for the jury how they had been drawn into, directly or indirectly, the murder case that was now before them. Martha Chamberlin, the maid, told how she had found Kathryn's body. Officer James Randolph Ellis explained how he had been called to the Valley River Inn on a report of a dead body. Detectives Lloyd Davis and David Poppe described how they had entered the case, and outlined their investigation of the murder. Molly Griggs told how she had met Lissy, how he had solicited her help in finding a hit man, to no avail, and how she had helped break the case wide open for the police. And on it went. The case unfolded just like a television movie of the week, and held the spectators and jurors spellbound. But, of course, everyone realized that this wasn't some fictional mystery that they were watching on television. This was real life.

"Call Beth Cumley!" Deputy District Attorney Brian Barnes commanded. Beth, by now twenty-three and happily married, quietly took the stand. Under direct examination, she answered Barnes's questions in a voice so soft that she had to be asked several times to speak up so that everyone in the courtroom could hear her. But despite her hushed tones, she held nothing back. She described how she had met Lissy, worked for him at the scuba-diving shops, and had performed sexual acts on him for money. Like he had done with Molly Griggs, Beth explained how Lissy had approached her to find a hit man for him and how she had resisted those efforts.

"You first met Mr. Lissy in 1982," Lissy's attorney, Ronald Sticka, stated during cross-examination. "Can you be any more specific than that?"

"It was—I can't recall, (I) believe it was the later part of eighty-two," Beth testified.

"Where did that meeting occur?" Sticka asked.

"At Just for the Health of It, hot-tubbing, downtown Portland," Beth answered.

"Were you working down in this area at the time?"

"No, I wasn't working down there."

"Was this just a casual meeting?"

"No . . . my friend set it up."

"As a professional-type meeting?"

"What do you mean?"

"Was this to be set up as sex for money?"

"Yes."

Beth explained how she began working for Lissy in May 1983. But prior to going to work for him at one of the scuba shops, she said she had met frequently with Lissy for the purpose of providing him with sex for money. During one of those sexual trysts, Lissy asked her if she wanted a job.

"Did you ask for the job?" Sticka asked.

"No," she replied. "He told me he needed a new person, that the person he had wasn't doing a well enough job."

"As for the sex for money, how much would you be paid each time?"

"Fifty dollars."

"Fifty dollars," Sticka repeated. "How much were you making at the scuba shop?"

"Started out making four dollars an hour," she said. "I went up to five."

"Were you working full-time?"

"Pretty much."

"And what type of work were you doing?"

"I was cleaning up both scuba shops," she said. "I would answer phones. I did everything. I took merchandise back and forth from each store."

"You handled retail sales?"

"Yes, I did sales, too."

"So you had access to the cash register?" Sticka asked. The question seemed like it might have been intended to serve as an opening for him to perhaps explain away some of the money that had been taken out of Lissy's business, perhaps to even find a scapegoat for why the books couldn't be balanced. But Sticka didn't persist in that direction. He just let the question linger, even after Beth answered.

"Yeah," she said. "There wasn't really a cash register. It was just a box there."

"Did you do any cleaning of the apartment or the condominium where Mr. Lissy stayed?"

"Yes."

"Both places?"

"Both places."

"Had you met Kathryn Martini-Lissy?"

"Yes."

"Was she down at the store very frequently?"

"She came in and out."

"And did you see her at the condominium?"

"Yeah."

"Did any of these sexual liaisons occur at the apartment?" Sticka asked.

"Yes."

"Over what period of time?"

"The whole period of time."

"Where else?"

"Well, there was a couple times in the scuba store."

"Anywhere else?"

"At the condominium."

"Isn't it true that Elise Dunn lived in the apartment across the street (from the scuba shop)?"

"Yes."

"Was she involved in any of those (trysts)?"

"No."

"Was she present when you and Mr. Lissy were at the apartment?"

"No."

"When was the last time you had contact with Mr. Lissy?"

"It was after Kathy had died, he called me . . . and told me that Kathy had been murdered. I knew that was it. I didn't want anything more to do with him because I knew that he had done it."

"When was the last time you saw Kathy?" Sticka asked.

"It must have been a couple of weeks before, at the scuba shop, I believe."

"Was Elise Dunn there at the time?"

"I don't recall."

"Ever see the two of them together?"

"Yes."

"How did they get along?" Sticka asked.

"They seemed to get along all right."

It didn't seem to be the answer Sticka had hoped for, but he stayed with the approach. It appeared that he was trying to cast a shadow on Elise, perhaps open another avenue for the jury to consider.

"How well did you know Elise?"

"I didn't know her well. I just knew her from coming into the store. I didn't really like her very much, so I tried to stay clear, you know."

"You didn't like Elise very much?"

"No. She had a bad temper."

"Kind of explosive-type person?"

"Yeah . . . I could work with her. I could tolerate her, but as far as getting to know her, being friends, it wasn't what I wanted."

"When Kathryn was not there at the shop, did Elise ever say anything about Kathryn Lissy?"

"No, not to me, really." From her tone, it appeared that Beth had caught on to what the attorney was driving at.

Having failed to implicate Elise in Lissy's plotting, Sticka returned to his original strategy, namely to convince the jury that Lissy's plotting amounted to nothing more than a form of bragging to impress his street friends that he was capable of killing someone, that it was all a game, a fantasy that he was playing inside his own mind.

"So . . . out of the blue . . . he asks you if you can get a hot gun or something to that effect?" Sticka asked.

"Yeah, he told me he needed a gun . . . wanted to get a hot gun."

"Did he say why he needed it?"

"Because he was afraid . . . of this man that was supposedly following him. I don't know if there was somebody really following him . . . I wasn't sure."

"Had you seen anyone following him?"

"No."

"You ever see Mr. Lissy act like anyone was following him?" Sticka asked.

"He had been acting very strange at the time."

"In what way?"

"He was very hard to get a hold of, staying away from the shops."

"Like he was hiding out or something?"

"Yeah."

It seemed like Sticka wanted to present a picture of a Lissy who wanted very much to appear like a big shot of sorts to his street friends. That's why he brought up certain aspects of Lissy's background. But he had to be careful at the same time. He didn't want Lissy's lies, his deceit, to come across as part of any plot to commit fraud. He wanted the untruths to seem to the jury like Lissy was only nurturing his ego, telling stories to impress people, an extension of a fantasy he was playing out with his street friends.

"Mr. Lissy told you a lot of stories, didn't he?" Sticka asked.

"Yeah."

"Did he tell you he was a graduate of Harvard or anything of that nature?"

"Yeah, he said that, I believe."

"Did you believe him when he told you that?"

"Yes."

"Did he tell you about his work for the State Department?"

"No. He mentioned something about doing diving for National Geographic, but nothing about the State Department."

"You believed him when he told you that he worked for National Geographic?"

"I wasn't sure about that."

"Did he tell you he was an ambassador to an African country?"

"No."

"He never told you that?"

"No."

"Did he tell you he was doing big drug deals?"

"No."

"But isn't it true he would tell you stories? You didn't know whether to believe him or not?"

"Yeah, some stories I did, some stories I didn't."

On redirect, Barnes made every effort to get the jury's focus back on Lissy as a fraud and a schemer of the worst sort. He wanted the jury to see Lissy for what he knew him to be.

"The last time he talked about Kathy . . . prior to her death . . . what was that conversation?"

"He talked to me when I went to clean up the apartment," Beth said. "He said that he was going to leave Kathy and stay at the apartment and get back with Elise."

"Did, in your presence, he ever indicate that his wife was aware that he was having sex for fees with you and others?"

"No."

"As far as you know, he utilized that apartment across from the scuba shop on Barbur to meet for sexual liaisons with other prostitutes?"

"Yes."

"Were you a prostitute at that time?"

"No."

"You were just recruited into this by your girl-friend?"

"Yes."

"Have you ever worked on the streets of Port-land?"

"Not on the streets, no."

"This friend of yours, was she a prostitute that introduced you to him, an acquaintance?"

"She was."

"Prior to the time that he asked you about getting a hot gun and getting a hit man, appar-ently mid-June, had you already done something for him that was of a criminal nature?"

"Yes, I did."

"And just get down to it," Barnes urged. "Did that involve the scuba shop?"

"Yes. He wanted to collect on insurance," Beth said.

At that point, Judge Beckett intervened to make certain that Beth was aware of her consti-tutional rights against self-incrimination. At first she didn't want to proceed without consulting an attorney, and exercised her Fifth Amendment rights. However, after a few moments of thought and without having any promises made to her that she wouldn't be prosecuted, she decided to go ahead and testify.

"You are doing this freely and voluntarily?" Beckett asked.

"Yes."

"Okay, proceed," Beckett said, after he was

satisfied that Beth had waived her Fifth Amendment rights.

"What were you doing for this insurance money that the defendant was talking to you about?" Barnes asked.

"We had to remove equipment, Elise and I," Beth answered. "Michael instructed us to remove it . . . do a fake robbery so he could collect on the insurance money . . . and put it in the storage." The faked robbery, she said, had occurred in the autumn of 1983.

"How much did you get for that?"

"I didn't get anything for it."

"He promised to give you some money?"

"Yes, he said he'd give me five hundred dollars."

"And when would he pay you that money?"

"After he received insurance money."

Beth explained that Lissy, sometime later, had told her that he had made a claim for the "loss," but stated that the insurance company wasn't buying it. Instead of paying the claim, they were investigating it.

"Did he refer to another insurance fraud during your conversation with him?" Barnes asked. The defense, Barnes contended, had opened the door to that line of questioning with Lissy's "tall-tale recollections." Barnes was just pushing it the rest of the way open.

"Yes. He said that they—he and Elise—had done another one prior, at the apartment they lived in. They had stolen their own equipment, furniture, and everything, and claimed it."

"Were you afraid of Mr. Lissy?"

"Yes, I was."

Beth explained that she was afraid that Lissy would expose the sexual relationship she was having with Lissy to her fiancé, and that is why she agreed to help Lissy carry out the fraudulent robbery of one of his scuba shops. Barnes quickly turned the subject back to Kathy's life insurance.

"Do you recall the context in which Lissy said that Kathy had no insurance?" Barnes asked.

"Yes. He told me that she had no insurance when he called to tell me that she was dead, and he told me that the first thing when I went to the funeral . . . funeral was held at the condominium, in the main hall . . . I walked in and they were standing there in line . . . I walked in and mingled . . . the minute he saw me, he started crying and the first thing he said to me was that she didn't have any insurance . . . it just struck me as real odd he would say that when, you know, we were at her funeral . . . afterwards he didn't know what to do because he was going to have to sell everything."

"That is the context?"

"That was the context of the last conversation we had. She had no insurance. He had to sell the house. He was going to sell the car and the condo and everything . . . I was very suspicious at that point. The minute he mentioned insurance, I *knew,* I had a feeling. . . ."

"Did he indicate anything to you in respect to his sexual relationship with Elise?" Barnes asked.

"As far as I knew, they were still seeing each other."

"How did you know that?"

"Because he said so."

"And by 'seeing each other,' what do you mean?"

"He was going over there to the apartment and spending time with Elise."

"Did (the defense investigator) suggest anything to you about Elise?"

"He suggested that she may have influenced Michael in something to do with the murder. And I told him that if anybody influenced anybody, it was Michael influencing everybody else."

Twenty-four

One by one police and law enforcement support witnesses took the stand to testify to their findings in Kathryn Martini-Lissy's death. Dr. Edward F. Wilson, Lane County Medical Examiner, clinically explained how he had determined the cause and probable time of Kathy's death during the autopsy.

"Assuming that there is evidence that the victim last ate dinner, consisting of prime rib and vegetables, had two glasses of wine, and this occurred during the period between six-thirty and seven-thirty P.M. on the fifth of July, 1984, based upon your autopsy and that additional data, are you able to state within some range the probable time of death?" Barnes asked.

"The estimate would be that this woman died within a few hours, one to two hours after she ate," Wilson said.

"Can you tell the jury generally how that is done?"

Wilson explained, that is the length of time it takes for the food to pass from the stomach to the small intestine, and would be used as a standard in a death investigation, particularly if the time of the person's last meal was known.

"You can follow this in a stomach and see how quickly it leaves the stomach . . . and then you look at the contents of the stomach and try to figure out if it is all in the stomach, if some passed on to the . . . duodenum, small intestine," Dr. Wilson continued. Wilson explained that in an average, healthy person the process of the food leaving the stomach normally takes from four to six hours. In Kathy's case, much of her last known meal was still in her stomach which, of course, meant that she had to have died before four to six hours had elapsed from the time that she had eaten dinner. The jury saw that Dr. Wilson's estimate of Kathy's time of death certainly fit neatly within the time frame that the police believed David Wilson and Gretchen Schumacher arrived in Eugene on the night of the murder.

When Detective Edward Van Horn was called to testify, he explained his contact with Molly Griggs in Portland on the night of July 12, 1984, following Griggs's meeting with Lissy in which he had passed money to her presumably to buy her silence.

"Did you obtain anything from her?" Barnes asked.

"Yes, I did," Van Horn replied.

"Witness be shown State's Exhibits Ten and Eleven, please? Looking at Ten, tell us if you recognize what Ten is."

"This is money that I removed from Molly Griggs's purse on that evening."

"How did you remove it?"

"I removed it with my fingertips and then placed it into this envelope without going through and counting it and sealed the envelope, initialed it," Van Horn said.

"Why did you proceed in that manner?"

"So I could submit the money to our police-department crime lab so it could be processed for fingerprints."

"You recognize one of the bills in the packet as being different (from how) it was originally?"

"Yes, I do."

"Is that the one in the plastic envelope?"

"Yes, it is."

"And you recognize the substance on that bill?"

"Yes, I do."

"What is it?"

"It is similar to discoloration caused by a process to obtain fingerprints."

"That wasn't like that when you obtained it?" Barnes asked.

"No, it was not."

"Who did you give those bills to?"

"I turned them over to Don Schuessler, a member of our police-department crime lab."

"State's Exhibit Eleven, do you recognize what is depicted there?"

"Yes, I do."

"Tell us about that."

"These are photographs taken in the motel room at the Portland Motor Lodge, showing the money inside of Molly Griggs's purse, and then photographs showing me removing the money from her purse and placing it into this manila envelope."

"Don Schuessler, please . . . what is your occupation?" Barnes asked after Schuessler was seated in the witness-box and duly sworn.

Schuessler explained that he had processed the pillowcase seized from Kathy's hotel room for latent fingerprints. It had some blood on it, but he was unable to develop any prints from it. He did, however, remove some hairs from the pillow, which he turned over to the Oregon State Police Crime Laboratory in Eugene. Similarly, he processed the matchbook found on the bed near Kathy's body and obtained one partial latent print, but not enough of the print was present to establish identification. There were no prints at all on the ashtray that they had found on the bed.

"How about the purse, then?" Barnes asked.

"The purse was processed for latent prints and also sent to the FBI laboratory in Washington, D.C., for laser examination," Schuessler said. Laser examination, he explained, was simply a scanning technique using laser light. If fingerprints are present, they will fluoresce under the laser light and are photographed for use in comparison with prints of a known suspect. "Both of the examinations came up negative, however," he added.

"Did you also examine the sunglasses, comb, and some other papers and such in the room?"

"Yes, sir, I did."

"And what were the results?"

"They were all negative."

"The witness be shown State's Exhibit Ten and Twelve, please? Would you look first at Number Twelve and tell us if that is something you recognize?"

"Yes, sir, it is," Schuessler replied.

"What is it?"

"A fingerprint card that I rolled of Mr. Lissy's fingerprints on September twenty-seventh of last year, during grand-jury proceedings."

"Did you have occasion to compare what you found on the card of the defendant's prints with State's Exhibit Number Ten, or any part of it?" State's Exhibit Ten, of course, was the envelope of money taken from Molly Griggs's purse.

"Yes, sir, I did."

"What part of it?"

"With State's Exhibit Number Ten, I first processed the money for latent fingerprints. And during the processing, I found a print that was suitable for comparison on a fifty-dollar bill."

"Is that the one within plastic?"

"Yes, it is."

"What did you do then?"

"I compared the fingerprint on the fifty-dollar bill to the known prints of Mr. Lissy."

"And what conclusion did you reach?"

"The fingerprint on the fifty-dollar bill was made by the left ring finger of Mr. Lissy."

"Any doubt in your mind about that?"

"No."

"This is a positive identification?"

"Yes, sir."

"I have no further questions," Barnes said. Following a brief cross-examination of the witness by Ronald Sticka, in which the total number of points of identification of a single fingerprint were discussed, Barnes called Detective David Poppe to testify.

"Detective Poppe, I'm going to direct your attention specifically to the thirteenth of July, 1984," Barnes stated. "Were you asked by a supervisor to do something particular in reference to Mr. Lissy?"

"Yes," Poppe answered. "I returned a call to Mr. Lissy."

Barnes asked the clerk to show Poppe State's Exhibit Eight, the court approved tape recording of the telephone conversation between Poppe, Davis, and Lissy.

The tape recording was then played for the jury, after which Sticka began his cross-examination of Poppe.

"I think you were only present during the

first, or prior to the first, telephone conversation with Molly. Is that correct?" Sticka asked.

"Yes," Poppe replied.

"Who handled the investigation from that close-controlled standpoint?"

"I was ordered back to Eugene. I know that Sergeant Hill had the major responsibility when I left."

"Your apparent involvement in discussions to set up the situation with Molly Griggs then was confined to the first day. Is that correct?"

"That's correct."

"And isn't it true, as part of those discussions, the effort was to create an impression in Mr. Lissy's mind that he was being contacted by an individual who represented she had possibly incriminating information or compromising information against Mr. Lissy. She was trying to get some money from Mr. Lissy, something to that effect?"

"That's roughly accurate," Poppe said. "Although the plan involved giving her a theme and having her say she was scared, had some information, and getting a reaction—a statement or reaction from him. That might include money—we didn't know when we started."

"But it was to confront Mr. Lissy with the fact that she had information, and unless he could help, she would go to the police. Wasn't that part of the discussion?"

"Yes, that's definitely part of it, although part

of it was playing it by ear. We didn't know what his reaction would be."

"(Did) he say he was innocent?"

"Among other things."

"That's all," Sticka said.

"I guess to make it clear," argued Barnes on redirect, "did he ever, at any other time, tell you that this was Molly Griggs he talked to?"

"No," Poppe stated.

"Molly, instead of 'Holly'?"

"No, he did not."

"Did he ever mention that this person that he referred to as 'Holly' had called him up and indicated she had incriminating evidence about the plan to kill his wife?"

"No."

"He ever indicate to you, or did you ever hear on tape at any other stage, a conversation (between Molly and Lissy) . . . wherein the mention of Mr. Sturgeon was made by the defendant?" Barnes was driving home the point that Lissy had told Davis and Poppe in the taped telephone conversation between them that he had told the woman, "Holly," to contact his attorney, and had then hung up. But the reference to the attorney was not present on the tapes of the conversations between Lissy and Molly.

"No."

"Did he tell you at any later time that he really knew who that (Molly or Holly) was?"

"No."

"So the only information he gave you about

the person that was supposedly trying to blackmail him, i.e., *Holly with an H,* was that contained on the phone call?" He was referring to
the recorded phone call that Poppe and Davis
had made to Lissy.

"That is correct."

"You knew that that information, at that time,
was false?"

"Yes."

"Nothing further," Barnes said.

"I don't know if you ever worked vice detail
or had a lot of contact with prostitutes," Sticka
said on recross.

"I have worked vice," Poppe stated.

"You have worked vice. Is it your common
perception that prostitutes use names other than
their own?"

"That's not uncommon."

"Isn't it true that they frequently *do* use names
not their own?"

"That is true."

"Did you ever do an inquiry on Molly Griggs
to find out if she ever went by any other name
on the streets?" Sticka was reaching.

"No, I haven't," Poppe said.

"You never made that inquiry, did you?"
Sticka drove the point home for the jury's benefit.

"I have talked to a number of street people

who said they knew her by that name, 'Molly,' "
Poppe said.

"That was the name she gave them?"

"Yes, and asked if they knew who this person
was."

"Did you make an inquiry down there about
anyone named 'Holly'?"

"No, I didn't."

After Sticka finished, Barnes asked Poppe one
final question.

"Did the defendant tell you, on the thirteenth,
when you called him, that just the day before
he didn't even know who this hooker was, but
paid her three hundred dollars?"

"No, he did not (mention the $300)," Poppe
said.

"That was part of your reasons for not trust-
ing his word?"

"Yes."

"That's all."

James Otto Pex, a criminalist with the Oregon
State Police Crime Lab in Eugene, testified regarding hair and trace evidence that had been
collected from Room 305 at the Valley River Inn.
Barnes asked him to examine State's Exhibits
Twenty-two and Twenty-three, Exhibit Twenty-
two being hair and debris collected at the crime
scene, and Exhibit Twenty-three being hair standards collected from individuals by court order
during the grand-jury proceedings.

"Did you attempt to make some comparisons with hair found on items allegedly removed from the victim's room, with hairs of other persons that were known?" Barnes asked.

"Yes. I had the head and pubic hairs reportedly from Kathryn Ann Martini-Lissy," Pex replied. "And I also had head hairs, moustache hairs, beard hairs, and pubic hairs from David Dean Wilson."

"Did you have any from the defendant?"

"Not that I know of. None were submitted to our laboratory."

"What were your findings in respect to the hairs that were seized from the room?"

"One of the exhibits, which was labeled Debris and Hair Found from the Bedspread, contained several hairs that were similar to Martini-Lissy's head hair and pubic hair, and also there were two pubic hairs which I found to be similar that could have come from Wilson. Also there was a hair that was picked from a pillowcase, which was similar to Martini-Lissy's . . . we also observed hairs that could not be accounted for."

Under Sticka's cross-examination, Pex explained that the method of examination used to determine similarities between hair characteristics was called comparison microscopy. He described a microscope equipped with one binocular eyepiece and two stages. A hair strand of possible evidentiary value can be placed on one of the two stages, and a hair strand taken from a suspect can be placed on the other stage so that both hairs can be viewed microscopically, side by side.

"We can see both of them at the same time," Pex said, "and of course we can adjust the magnification to look at the microscopic detail which is in the hairs. Human hairs are semitransparent, and you can see within them."

"Could you identify hairs of David Wilson as, in fact, being on the premises in Room 305?" Sticka asked.

"Is it an absolute identification?"

"It is not, is it?" Sticka asked.

"It is not an absolute identification," Pex admitted, "but with microscopic examination you can see the characteristics of the hairs, whether your questioned hair fits within the biological variance of David Wilson. But as you look around the room, you see that you would think that everyone would have fairly unique hair, because a whole head of hair is fairly unique. But there are biological variances that do tend to overlap. That is why the report says they are similar and could have originated from him. He cannot be excluded."

"In other words, those hairs could have come from another individual. Is that correct?"

"That is hypothetically possible, yes," Pex answered.

"Is it your understanding that hairs that you received were all of the hairs seized within the room as a result of vacuuming and/or other methods of retrieval?" Sticka asked. He pointed out that several of the hairs found in Room 305 were not similar to the hairs seized from Wilson and from Kathy's body.

"I have to go by my personal experience in doing crime-scene processing," Pex answered. "And it is highly unlikely you could seize every hair that is in the room."

"From your general experience, would you expect to find a lot of unidentified hairs in a room such as a motel room?"

"I would expect to find some," Pex said.

Twenty-five

"What town are you from, Mr. Franklin?" Barnes asked Bary Franklin, twenty-three.

"Portland," Franklin replied.

"How long have you lived there?"

"All my life, twenty-three years."

"Have you had occasion, during your living there, to meet Michael Lissy?"

"Yes, I have," he replied.

"Whereabouts did you meet him?"

"By my house, Twenty-first and Northwest Flanders."

Responding to Barnes's questions, Franklin told the jury that he had met with Lissy on at least four occasions prior to June 1984. In the latter part of June of that year, Franklin said that Lissy had called him at home. Lissy wanted to meet him out someplace, to talk to him about some "business." Franklin explained that the "business" was that Lissy wanted someone killed.

"Just a minute," Barnes said. "I want to set the stage a little bit. Where did you meet?"

"He came by my place and I met him outside," Franklin testified. "And we went for a ride."

They went for the ride in Kathy's car, Franklin said, and they talked. Lissy told him that he had a problem with his wife, his ex-wife, and his ex-wife's boyfriend. He had claimed that they were taking merchandise out of his scuba shops. Lissy had wanted his wife, Kathy, killed, and Elise's boyfriend severely beaten and possibly killed.

"He wanted to set it up like it was a drug deal," Franklin said. "And he wanted her killed and her purse taken so that it looked like it was a robbery."

"How was the killing actually going to happen?" Barnes asked.

"It was by pistol."

According to Franklin, Lissy was to convince Kathy to meet Franklin about a supposed drug deal on a street in Northwest Portland only blocks from Franklin's house.

"She would meet me and in her car I was supposed to hit her at this spot . . . I was supposed to kill her and take her purse and make it look like a robbery," Franklin said.

"Did you meet with him again?"

"Yes . . . on the next meeting we talked about it a little more, and he gave me nine hundred dollars and a .357 magnum pistol, short nose," said Franklin.

"What was the gun for?" Barnes asked.

"To kill her."

"And the money?"

"Payment on killing her."

"Was nine hundred dollars an agreed upon figure?"

"No," Franklin replied. "One thousand dollars was. Another hundred would be delivered later because he was having money problems."

Barnes had the court clerk bring out the gun, State's Exhibit Fifteen, consisting of the gun, holster and bullets recovered during a legal search of Lissy's home and van. Franklin stated that the exhibited materials appeared similar to the ones he received from Lissy.

Franklin explained that he and Lissy met again, possibly their third or fourth meeting, at which time Franklin told him that he was not going to kill his wife for him. He said that he told Lissy that it would "be crazy" for him to get involved in something like that, and he returned the gun and the money to him.

"He was very upset," Franklin said. "His face turned red. It was like he was under a great deal of pressure."

"Did he ever act like he was joking?"

"No, definitely not."

Under cross-examination, Sticka asked pointed questions about Franklin's life in an attempt to discredit him as a reliable witness in the jury's eyes. He also tried to demonstrate, to no avail, that Franklin didn't know the difference between Lissy's ex-wife Elise and his wife Kathy. It was a typical defense move in a trial such as this.

"Mr. Franklin, you have a prior conviction, do you not?" Sticka asked.

"Yes, I do."

"That is theft in the first degree?"

"Yes."

"That is a felony, isn't it?"

"Yes."

"And by your testimony, seriously entertained and accepted a plan for killing someone for one thousand dollars?"

"No. I never accepted it."

"You talked to Mr. Lissy like you were serious about it?"

"Yes, I did."

"Why did you do that?"

"Because I was going to take the nine hundred dollars and the .357 magnum, sell the gun, and keep the money, because he couldn't tell the police."

"As far as the gun identification you made, how many .357 magnums have you seen?" Sticka asked.

"Since my father is a collector of guns, I have seen quite a few," Franklin said.

"You have one at the time?"

"No, I didn't."

"You don't have any guns?"

"No."

"Because of your status with your probation or anything?"

"Yeah, I am on probation."

"You weren't supposed to have a gun?"

"No."

"You haven't violated probation, have you?"

"No, I haven't," Franklin said. "I might jeopardize it by coming here today, so I have to take the chance."

"Are you expecting that action is going to be taken against you because of your appearance here today?"

"Well, I don't know. That's up to the probation authorities."

"You are hopeful they won't take any action?"

"Yes."

"Is there anything about the particular gun that makes it different from any other .357 magnum?"

"Basically, you don't see too many .357s with a rubber handle on it," Franklin replied. "I remember that because it is a fingerprint-proof grip . . . it is chrome plated."

"Have you ever gone into a gun store to see what kind of guns they have?"

"Yes."

"Have you ever seen any like that in there?"

"No."

"And you said you recognized the bullets, too?"

"Yes."

"Something unusual about those bullets?"

"Yeah, hollow nose."

"Have you ever seen hollow-nose bullets before?"

"Yes, I have."

"Not too unusual, are they?"

"They are unusual to see somebody carrying around," Franklin said.

Sticka brought the bullets over for Franklin to look at again, and asked him if he could testify that they were the same bullets that Lissy had brought him with the gun. Franklin, of course, couldn't swear that they were the same ones that Lissy brought him. They only looked like the same bullets.

"Was there anything distinctive about the gun, other than it was a .357 magnum with rubber grips?" Sticka asked.

"The holster."

"What do you remember about the holster?"

"Well, it looks like it happens to be a shoulder holster, but it doesn't have any straps on it," Franklin said. "So that is why I recognize the holster again."

Sticka turned Franklin's testimony toward Elise Dunn's boyfriend, Brad Lemmer: "Starts out one person, then there is some discussion about that, then all of a sudden two people are involved?"

"Yes."

"That was really starting to get you a little nervous about what was going on there?" Sticka asked.

"The man, I felt (him) to be very unstable."

"Is that because he throws in another intended, supposed victim at you?"

"Yes."

"That is what concerned you, is that correct?"

"No."

"That didn't concern you?"

"It concerned me that this man is going around wanting people dead," Franklin retorted. Franklin explained that he had never seen Elise's boyfriend, and Lissy had never shown him a photo of him. However, he and Lissy, driving in Lissy's blue van, drove to Brad Lemmer's place of employment, a Chrysler-Plymouth dealership in Northeast Portland. "Lissy said, 'This is where the man works.'"

Elise Dunn testified that she was Michael Lissy's ex-wife and had been the bookkeeper for his scuba business. She characterized Lissy as an often violent man with an explosive temper who spent large sums of money, siphoned from the business, on prostitutes. She said that he had a strong sexual appetite that required unusual, sometimes sadistic, and group sexual acts. She told the jury that he had continued to use the services of prostitutes after his marriage to Kathy, whom he often referred to as "the dragon lady."

"Did he, throughout the contact with you, continually indicate that he wasn't involved in her death?" Barnes asked.

"Yes, he did."

"At one point did he use a particular phrase to describe himself and his innocence?"

"He said he was a chickenshit liar. He said he would not do anything that obvious."

"On the twenty-fifth of September, did you have some conversation with him, or about that time?"

"Yes, I did. I had been subpoenaed for the grand jury."

"Did you talk with the defendant about his being subpoenaed?"

"Yes, I did. He said he had been subpoenaed. He was calling me from his parents' residence at the beach. Gretchen had been subpoenaed, and . . . he was very concerned about what she would say. And he said he was concerned about a person named Molly, that they had some type of recording of he and Molly."

"On the tenth of August, did you have a conversation with him?" Barnes asked.

"Yes, I did. Several."

"Without getting into what the stories were, did he indicate anything in respect to what his intent was in telling certain stories?"

"He said that the reason for circulating stories about killing me, killing his other family members, killing my husband (then boyfriend), are to cloud the issue of Kathy's death . . . he said he was scared . . . he was trying to bullshit everybody."

"Is that a quote?"

"That's a quote."

Elise explained how Lissy had asked her to underreport his sales income by $5,000 in June and $2,000 in July. She also said that Lissy had married Kathy only because his attempts to obtain a loan through her banking connections had failed. But, she said, if he married Kathy, "Kathy's father would give him a loan and that's why he had to marry her." She told of how Lissy had promised to come back to her and remarry her after he obtained the money he needed to save his fast-failing business. She also told the jury about the piece of paper with "305" written on it that he had asked her to destroy. "I thought it connected Michael Lissy with the murder—it was Kathy's room number."

She said that she had participated in some of Lissy's earlier schemes, such as robbing their own apartment and removing equipment from the scuba shop to make it look like a burglary because of her fear of him.

"I was afraid of what he would do to me if I did not participate. I was afraid of losing him . . . I didn't want to lose him. He told me that I was so undesirable I'd never find another man. He was the best I would ever find. I was insecure, and he knew how to use that. He could get quite physical, and I was afraid of what would happen to me if I disobeyed him . . . I was afraid of being beaten by him . . . beaten, sodomized, raped . . . I was terrified of the man."

Elise explained how Lissy had convinced her to go to work at a massage parlor, in addition to holding down her regular job as an accountant due to a financial mess that Lissy had gotten her into. "When—in that period of your life where you went into the massage parlor, was that your idea?" Barnes asked.

"No, it wasn't."

"Tell us how you got there. What were the conversations you had with Mr. Lissy about your choices then?"

"He wasn't making the loan payment to me. And since the money came directly out of my checks at work, my take-home pay was about four hundred dollars and it is kind of hard to live on that. He suggested that I become a dancer at a topless bar, and I refused. Then he suggested that I become a prostitute and he would be my pimp and I would walk the streets, and I refused. And then he suggested the massage business."

"Why did you do that?"

"Because I needed money to eat on."

"And did you think that was a lesser of evils?"

"Lesser of the three evils, yes."

On the day that Lissy told Elise about Kathy's death, she and Lissy had gone for a drive together. They stopped at a store so that he could buy some crossword puzzles, then they drove to a Häagen-Dazs and had ice cream. Sometime later they found a vacant parking lot where they stopped for a while. The encounter between Elise and Lissy occurred on Saturday, July 7, the day after Kathy's body was discovered.

"Was he driving?" Barnes asked.

"No, I was driving."

"How did you happen to stop?"

"He asked me to perform oral sex."

"Was he—did he appear upset or grief stricken?"

"Not at that time."

"Did that act occur?"

"No, it did not."

Elise related an incident that occurred between her and Lissy in August 1984, nearly two months before Lissy's arrest but well after he knew that the cops were onto him. Lissy, she said, had offered to pay her for favorable testimony in court. He had said that she "was the only one who could nail him . . . he offered me ten thousand dollars to make him look nice."

She testified that Lissy often required sex of a "more varietal nature than I liked." She described a time when he had suggested "threesomes" and "foursomes," even sex with a German shepherd. Although Elise said that she would have consented to his wishes in order to please him, the sex acts with a canine never occurred. She did, however, tell about one incident of group sex, a "threesome" that involved Tina LaPlante. That was the only time that Elise had been involved in group sex with Lissy, but Lissy continued to see prostitutes because "he said he needed variety."

"Did he suggest other unusual activities as well?" Barnes asked.

"He suggested a large black man, and he suggested a gorilla."

"Was he fantasizing at this time or—"

"I don't think so."

"Objection," Sticka interjected. "That question would call for a conclusion. Move the answer be stricken."

"Sustained," Beckett ruled.

"In respect to these, you already testified about threesomes. Is that right?" Barnes asked.

"That's right."

"Did those involve him?"

"Yes."

"At whose request?"

"At his request."

"Did you mean—I guess it depends on frame of reference—but animals and such would be oddities, but were there other things that were, I guess, average people might consider odd that did occur occasionally?"

"Yes, there were."

"What?"

"He performed anal sex and he liked golden showers." The anal sex, she said, was forcible, against her will.

"For the, I guess, education of those not familiar with this term, would you explain?"

"Golden showers are where the man stands over the woman and urinates on her."

"Did he ask you to do something special in reference to that type of activity on one occasion, and if so, so explain?"

"In October of eighty-three, my friends at work still did not know we were separated. I stopped wearing my wedding ring and just said we were having some problems. But I wanted to be able to tell them that we were reuniting, to wear the ring again. And he said in order for me to put my ring back on, not only would I have to have a golden shower, but I would have to swallow a mouthful."

"Did that, in fact, occur?"

"Yes, it did."

"How old were you when you met Mr. Lissy?"

"Twenty."

"Had you dated much at that time?"

"I had two or three steady boyfriends, but not much."

"How old is Mr. Lissy?"

"I believe he is thirty-five now."

"Did he introduce you to these types of sexual activities?"

"Yes, he did."

Elise told of one occasion when she drove Lissy and Kathy to the airport, when they were on their way to Belize, in which Kathy had told her about a letter that she had received in the mail that day. According to Elise, Kathy had said that the letter had asked something to the effect, "Do you know how many women Michael's fucking?"

When asked why Lissy hadn't just had an affair with Kathy, or perhaps only lived with her rather than getting married to her, Elise responded that a divorce was necessary because Kathy wasn't the type of woman to live with a married man. She was too classy for that, and worried how it would look to others. Nonetheless, Lissy didn't want Elise's family to know that they were getting divorced and went to great lengths to keep them from finding out. On one occasion he enlisted Elise's help to bring that scheme off.

"He didn't want my family to know that he was getting married so that when we reunited, it would seem like we hadn't really been apart that long, or hadn't been that serious. He had me call *The Oregonian* after the wedding and tell them I was Kathy Martini and to say that the wedding had been called off, and to please not print the wedding notice in the paper." *The Oregonian* complied, she said. "I checked the paper. It wasn't in there."

According to Elise's testimony, within days after Kathy's death she and Lissy were meeting and engaging in sexual activity. Lissy, she said, hadn't appeared grief stricken.

"Were these the same sorts of sexual acts he performed previously?" Barnes asked.

"Yes, they were."

"You also described consenting to sexual acts when you were talking about being beaten and sodomized," Barnes stated.

"Maybe beaten isn't a correct term," Elise clarified. "He had a horsewhip he would use on me. I had welts all over my body. He wouldn't use it below my knees or on my face because then it would show and the women at work would know."

"Is that part of some kinky sex?"

"There was a time when he told me he needed to inflict pain in order to receive satisfaction for himself."

"I think that is where I will end it," Barnes said.

Paul McNeil testified about the fraud schemes and murder plots that he'd been involved in with Lissy. He told the jury basically the same things that he had told Davis and Poppe, including how he had helped Lissy transfer merchandise and money out of a convenience store that Lissy and Elise had managed. He also provided details of Lissy's home-burglary insurance-claim scheme, in which he and Lissy had moved several truck-loads of furniture and household appliances from Lissy and Elise's home to a rental storage unit, for which he had been paid with a nine-teen-inch color television.

McNeil also told about how he and Lissy had discussed plans to kill Lissy's elderly aunt for an inheritance and that he had "seemed detached, like it was someone else talking." They also had discussed plans to get Elise drunk and knock her off Lissy's sailboat to claim her life-insurance benefits, and they talked over a plan in which Kathryn would be given a drug overdose or arrange a fatal car accident for her in order to obtain her life-insurance benefits. McNeil said that he was to be paid with a sailboat for helping to kill Elise, and for helping with Kathy's murder, he said, he would have been paid approximately fifty percent of the insurance money.

"I think Kathryn had somewhere up in the quarter-million dollar figure in life insurance," McNeil testified that Lissy had told him. "He said that if she were out of town on business, the insurance would pay off better." However, McNeil said he never actually helped carry out the death plot, and therefore was not paid anything.

Lissy's mother, Patricia, weeping in the witness-box, backed her son. She told of how Lissy and Kathy had visited her and her husband, Ernest, at their home on the coast on July 1, five days before Kathy's body was found. They bought groceries and cooked dinner together for her and Ernest.

"It was the happiest day of my life because they were so happy," she said. She said that Lissy had been very happy with Kathy, and was grief stricken, "practically incoherent," when he learned of her death.

"He said if anything that he had said was responsible for this, he'd never forgive himself," Patricia said.

Patricia testified that Lissy had once brought her a fake list of his education and work credentials which showed that he had attended Harvard and Oxford universities, and that he had been employed by the U.S. State Department. The phony resume, which he had brought to her in June 1983, close to the time that he had met Kathy, had also made a reference to him having been an ambassador.

"Based on his reasons . . . he asked that upon meeting any of his friends or business associates, that I not say it wasn't so," she testified. Although Patricia discussed what her son's "reasons" had been for the deception, the jury was taken out of the courtroom and not allowed to hear them.

Lissy's stepfather, Ernest, also supported his adopted son. He said that Lissy was distraught and lacked control of his emotions when they met with him in Eugene on the evening of July 6. Ernest also testified that he and Patricia owned real estate holdings worth at least $700,000.

"He's not interested in waiting for someone to die to get their money," Ernest testified, relating how Lissy had told him that he wasn't interested in their will. Barnes, however, reminded the jury that the "old couple" on the coast that Lissy wanted killed because they were blocking a business deal were Lissy's parents.

Philip N. Barnhart, a psychologist who conducted interviews with Lissy and administered psychological tests on the defendant prior to the start of his trial, testified for the defense that Lissy suffered from personality disorders. According to Barnhart, Lissy was narcissistic, an habitual liar, and highly manipulative. On the surface Lissy was indifferent, but at the same time he was "driven by his need to be looked up to, to be either feared or respected by other people." Lissy's "fantasy" plots, Barnhart said, were consistent with his defense claims and Lissy's previous behavior.

"Mr. Lissy is a man who learned that the way to operate is to lie and engage in vast amounts of sexual activity and to fantasize with other people about things he'd like to do or things he has done," Barnhart said.

Twenty-six

When Lissy himself, appearing confident and at ease, was placed on the witness stand toward the end of his trial, he brazenly told the jury that the murder plans he was accused of participating in were nothing more than mere fantasized plots that he had constructed, just for kicks. The catch, he said, was that he never told his associates, the pimps and prostitutes that were his friends, that his plots were just a fantasy. If he had told them about his fantasy, he said, "Then there's no more game going on. If it's not real, people don't want to play."

"There had been two other plots and three other hit men (besides Wilson) that she'd (Tina LaPlante) brought to me—nothing ever happened," Lissy testified. "I don't think we ever backed out, it's just the time to do it expired . . . I've asked myself ten thousand times, why didn't you see it was going to happen? It just never did . . . it (the plotting) was a rush, you know, getting involved and all that. Is there a logical reason? No. It was just something I did.

"There was basically one plot but probably fifteen different people who had been involved in the plotting,'' Lissy continued. ''That Kathy would be killed in Eugene while on a business trip, at the Valley River Inn . . . I was hoping against hope and praying like hell that I wasn't involved,'' Lissy told the jury in describing his feelings when the police contacted him on July 6 to inform him that his wife had been murdered in Eugene. ''You can't talk about somebody dying and then have it happen and not wonder.''

''Would you lie to get off this murder charge?'' Deputy District Attorney Brian Barnes asked.

''I'm sure I probably would,'' Lissy replied. After thinking about what he'd just said, Lissy quickly changed his statement. ''I probably would have at one point—I wouldn't now . . . I've always, when I was cornered, used what I could.'' Lissy said that he'd been able to lie straight-faced for as long as he could remember.

''You'd do whatever you could to survive, wouldn't you?'' Barnes asked.

''That's right,'' Lissy replied. ''I lied repeatedly to the police. I did not want to be charged with the murder of my wife.'' Although Lissy said, ''I think I'm responsible for Kathy's death,'' he maintained throughout his trial that he had never intended for her to actually be killed. Instead, he said, the ''street people'' he associated with had taken it upon themselves to carry out the ''fantasy'' plots because they thought the plots were for real.

What about the large sums of money that he

had paid out? Barnes wanted to know. Lissy claimed the money was paid as bribes to keep Wilson and others quiet after the murder had occurred.

"Right afterward," Lissy said, "I paid a lot of bribes to people to keep quiet . . . it came down to paying off the people who were involved."

In summing up Lissy's defense to the jury, Sticka said that his client, although "morally despicable," was a victim like his dead wife, a victim of others who wanted to obtain money. Sticka said that Lissy's habitual fantasies of murder plots were transformed into reality by the pimps and prostitutes that he tried so hard to impress.

"It's the Walter Mitty syndrome," Sticka said. "He was living in a world of fantasy and could not determine the extent to which his behavior was dangerous," Sticka told the jury.

"So I submit what you have here is an unintended extension of the fantasy life of Michael Lissy," Sticka continued. "Never in any of these schemes has he ever intended the death of another human being . . . he's a victim of his own mouth."

As part of his closing arguments to the jury, Prosecutor Barnes replayed portions of the tape recordings of conversations that the police made between Lissy and Tina LaPlante, which included statements Lissy had made regarding the $25,000 he would pay David Wilson for "taking the fall" for Kathy's murder.

"The utter callousness of the defendant is illustrated on those tapes when Tina LaPlante asks him, 'Are you sorry?' and the defendant responds, 'No, are you?'," Barnes repeated. The mere fact that Kathy asked Wilson at the hotel, "Why is Michael setting me up?" demonstrated that Lissy had arranged for Wilson to come to her room, Barnes said. "It shows that she was aware of the situation set up by Michael Lissy which put her in a compromising position," he said, although Kathy didn't know that she was about to be killed.

"The defendant told us he's a liar—he said he might even lie to beat a murder case," Barnes said. "It's the biggest fraud of them all—a one-hundred-ninety-thousand-dollar insurance-fraud case. If the defendant was really grief stricken, so emotional about the death of his wife, was his reaction what you'd expect? Absolutely not," Barnes closed.

.The case was handed to the jury on Thursday, February 7, 1985.

After deliberating for only five-and-a-half hours, the nine-man, three-woman jury returned to the courtroom and announced that they had reached a verdict. The jury had unanimously found Michael David Lissy guilty of aggravated murder in the July 5, 1984, death of his wife. Lissy waived his right to a presentence investigation, and Lane County Circuit Judge William A. Beckett immediately sentenced Lissy to life in prison and imposed a thirty-year mandatory minimum sentence before Lissy could be eligible for parole. Since Oregon did not have a death penalty in 1985, a sentence of death was not an issue in sentencing Lissy. Lissy was promptly taken to the Oregon State Penitentiary in Salem to begin serving his sentence.

"We hoped he'd get the maximum and he did," one of Kathy's parents said to a reporter after the trial. "We wished he could have gotten the death penalty. With all the wonderful people in Oregon, Kathy had to meet the worst."

Epilogue

David Dean Wilson and Gretchen Marie Schumacher didn't waste any time. On Friday, February 8, 1985, the day after Lissy's conviction and sentence, Wilson and Schumacher both pleaded guilty to stipulated facts in their cases to avoid facing a trial by jury and potentially longer prison sentences. Wilson pleaded guilty to aggravated murder in connection with Kathryn Ann Martini-Lissy's death, and was sentenced by Lane County Circuit Court Judge George J. Woodrich to life in prison. Despite Wilson's guilty plea, however, Woodrich imposed a mandatory minimum sentence of twenty years before parole eligibility.

Gretchen pleaded guilty to conspiracy to commit murder and to first degree robbery before Judge Edwin E. Allen, to whom she admitted that she had driven Wilson to Eugene to commit the crimes. On paper, Gretchen was sentenced to forty years in prison, with no minimum sentence. But under parole board standards in effect at the time, such a sentence in reality meant that she could be paroled after serving as few as forty months. Though she remained in the Oregon Women's Correctional Facility in Salem longer than forty months, she is due to be paroled at the time of this writing.

Detective Lloyd Davis retired from the Eugene Police Department, and is currently living peacefully somewhere in the Eugene-Springfield area. David Poppe was promoted to sergeant and is still serving the citizens of Eugene.

Michael David Lissy, meanwhile, is still running scams from inside prison walls. Within a few months of being sentenced, Lissy became involved in a murder case that had occurred in Salem. According to authorities, Lissy reported that he had information about an ongoing murder investigation, details that he had heard from another inmate, and had tried to strike a deal with the state to reduce his prison term for his wife's murder. Marion County District Attorney Dale Penn almost went for a deal with Lissy. But due to persistent efforts by the Lane County District Attorney and Detectives Lloyd Davis and David Poppe to convince him that Lissy was a liar and was unreliabie, Penn turned down the deal. He ended up winning the case anyway, without Lissy's "help." Lissy, however, was quickly labeled a snitch and had to be transferred out of the Oregon prison system for his own safety. He is currently serving the remainder of his sentence at a northern California prison and, reportedly, is still scheming, looking for an early way out.